# For a moment, Faith felt the old pull.

"Sure," she said flatly. "Tell me about Suzanna."

Christopher reached out for Faith. "It's over. I told you I'd end it, and I did. Ask anybody. Didn't I tell you that you could trust me?"

Faith didn't fall for it this time. She pushed his arms away. "But I don't trust you, Christopher. How can I trust you when you've lied to me every step of the way?"

"I haven't lied to you! I broke off my engagement, just like I said I would. I did that for you."

"You didn't do that for me. You did that for the same person you do everything for—yourself."

For the first time all trace of ease and confidence left Christopher's face.

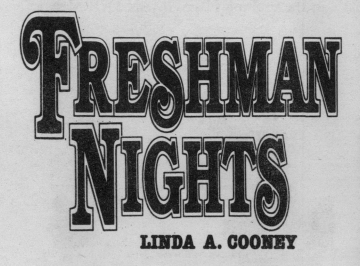

# FRESHMAN NIGHTS

### LINDA A. COONEY

## HarperPaperbacks

*A Division of HarperCollinsPublishers*

This is a work of fiction. The characters, incidents, and
dialogues are products of the author's imagination and are not
to be construed as real. Any resemblance to actual events or
persons, living or dead, is entirely coincidental.

HarperPaperbacks *A Division of* HarperCollins*Publishers*
                          10 East 53rd Street, New York, N.Y. 10022

Cover art by Tony Greco

First printing: December 1990

Printed in the United States of America

HarperPaperbacks and colophon are trademarks of
HarperCollins*Publishers*

10 9 8 7 6 5 4 3 2 1

# One

aith wasn't paying attention. Every time she tried to focus on something, thoughts of Christopher Hammond swirled in her brain.

"Faith, are you going to use that washing machine?"

"What, Winnie?"

"I'll use it," KC interrupted. "I should wash this dumb T-shirt more than once to make sure it looks like I've actually worn it."

"Throw it in with my stuff," Winnie joked. "Most of my clothes have been sitting in the bottom of my closet for so long, they look more than worn. They look digested."

KC laughed, and Faith turned away. It was Sunday night and the three best friends were doing laundry in the basement of Forest Hall, Winnie's dorm. Faith had her normal load of overalls and lacy blouses. KC was only concerned with her single, unworn T-shirt. Meanwhile, Winnie was sorting through nearly six weeks' worth of balled-up running tights, halter tops, boxer shorts, miniskirts, and day-glo sweaters.

"So, KC," Winnie chattered brightly, "what's the big deal with this T-shirt?" She held up the unworn tie-dyed shirt. It said, Presenting Kahia Cayanne Angeletti: University of Springfield Freshman Extraordinaire.

KC grabbed the T-shirt away and pitched it in with Faith's load of wash.

"Don't be so heartless, KC. I think the shirt is very you." Winnie laughed. "I can just see it with one of your blazers and dress-for-success skirts. Don't you think so, Faith?"

"Hm?" Faith glanced up from a washer and tossed back her braid. She stared at the machine's coin slot. She couldn't remember what she'd been doing. "Oh, sure, Win. Sure. It would look great. Anything looks great on KC."

"Look, Win," stated KC in a matter-of-fact voice, "my parents gave me that T-shirt as part of my high-school-graduation present." She shook her head, making her dark curls wobble. Her beautiful face looked as perfect as a cover girl's.

"So?"

"So I asked them for a briefcase and a computer. I got the briefcase, but instead of a computer I got a book on managing stress through health foods, plus that T-shirt." KC turned away and stuck two quarters in the candy machine.

Faith forced herself to get back into the conversation. "Maybe your parents couldn't afford a computer," she mentioned, breaking open a miniature box of soap. White powder spilled onto the concrete floor. "At least you got the briefcase."

"Faith, you are so nice—you always see the bright side," KC commented. "I just can't believe my hippie parents ever thought I'd like that T-shirt. As if I'd want to be seen in tie-dye, or have people know the ridiculous name they gave me."

"I like your real name." Winnie giggled. "It's exotic."

"Right. I can just see myself going in for some corporate job interview and saying, 'Like hi, my name is Kahia Cayanne.' "

"KC!" Winnie made a face, stretching her mouth and sticking out her tongue. "Where's your sense of humor?"

"A sense of humor, Winnie, is not what helps you get ahead." KC fished a chocolate bar out of the candy machine, then threw the wrapper in the trash.

Faith watched Winnie push quarters into a washer and made herself do the same. They plopped onto a bench and stared at the dryers, the mailboxes, the video game, and balls of lint. There was the sound of water being pumped into the machines and the lingering smell of bleach.

KC flung open her Intro to Business text, while Winnie bobbed to the beat on her Walkman. Faith thumbed the pages of a *Theatercrafts* magazine, staring at the words as if they were in a foreign language. Eventually the washing machines sped up, whirring away in spin cycle.

That was when Winnie whipped off her earphones and leaped up again. She waved her arms, making the ten-plus bracelets on each of her wrists jangle. "What's going on with you two?"

Faith pasted on a fake smile and stammered, "Nothing. I'm doing fine."

KC glared at her book.

"Why don't I believe you?" Winnie tossed back. "KC, I don't know if you realize it, but you are acting as if laundry were some demonic curse. And Faith, you keep saying everything is hunky-dory, but you're acting so spacey that you might as well be me. There is definitely something—or someone —on your mind. Maybe aliens invaded both of your bodies last night. You know, if I'd wanted a surreal experience, I could have done laundry by myself."

KC closed her textbook.

Faith put a hand to her forehead.

"Do you two want to know the Winnie Gottlieb theory on why you're both acting so weird?"

"Do we have to?" KC asked.

"That's one of the nice things about old friends. You always know what to expect. Okay. Here goes. The Gottlieb theory is . . ." Winnie posed in front of them, clapped her hands, and did a little dance. "We think we're so mature. I mean, here we are, college freshmen, each of us living in her own dorm —women of the nineties and all that. But all it takes is a tiny University of Springfield tradition called Parents' Visit and boingo!"

"Boingo?" KC questioned.

Faith lifted her head and tried to smile. A terrible, tight feeling was in her chest, as if her emotions had been cranked up so high and held in so hard that she just might explode.

"Yes," Winnie concluded. "The thought of our parents visiting us at college this week has turned us back into dorky, insecure little twelve-year-olds."

KC huffed. "Winnie, do you always have to talk so much?"

"Usually." Winnie respiked her already spiky hair with her fingers and continued, "Since I've made so many mistakes, I've earned the right to give advice. Now KC, you want your parents to think you've been wearing the shirt they gave you, so they won't hassle you about being so cold-hearted and ambitious."

"Gee, thanks, Win. Maybe you should declare a major in psychology."

"I'll leave the psychologizing to my mom." Winnie laughed. "Besides, I'm just as bad as you are. I cleaned my room this morning, for only the second or third time since orientation, because I don't want my mother to think I'm avoiding adult responsibilities. Plus, I don't want her analyzing the meaning of all those empty peanut-butter jars under my bed."

Faith rubbed her eyes. "Peanut-butter jars?"

"All we want is for our parents to come visit and think we're doing okay!" Winnie waited for a reply. "Well? Am I right? For once is crazy Winnie right?"

"You're not crazy." KC thought for a moment. "Actually, my problem is that I don't want my parents to come for this stupid Parents' Visit at all. I don't want to be seen with them."

"Your folks are great, KC," Winnie said. "Besides, everybody else will be so embarrassed by their own parents, they won't notice anyone else's. Faith, what about you?"

"Me?"

"Yeah," KC echoed. "What about you?"

Winnie and KC stared at Faith until she finally put her magazine back in her laundry bag and looked at them. Parents' Visit was something else she hadn't been able to concentrate on. "What about me?"

"You've always been so normal and happy and well adjusted," Winnie reasoned.

Faith cringed.

"But even super-normal Faith Crowley must be doing something psychotic to get ready for Parents' Visit," Winnie went on.

Faith let stray hairs fall over her delicate face. "I'm looking forward to seeing my folks. I miss them. My sister's coming too. I'm excited."

"You don't seem very excited," Winnie pointed out.

"I am. Just because I don't have to get rid of peanut-butter jars or pretend I wear clothes I don't really wear, that doesn't mean I'm not excited. Unlike you two, I have nothing to hide." As soon as Faith's words were out, she got that tight, exploding feeling again. She took more deep breaths, clenching and unclenching her fists as an uncomfortable silence filled the basement and the washing machines clunked to a halt.

"I never said you had something to hide," Winnie said softly.

Faith started to say something else, but thoughts and images of Christopher were filling her head. The pressure grew more and more painful as she held everything inside.

KC and Winnie began unloading the washers, pitching armloads of wet clothes into the dryers along the wall. Hiding her face from them, Faith hurried to the change machine. Soon the sound of tumbling clothes filled the basement again, accented by the hard *clack clack* of the clasps on Faith's overalls hitting the dryer's metal cylinder. The sound was like a hammer in Faith's head.

Meanwhile, Winnie chewed gum, hummed, and blew big bubbles. KC scanned a copy of the Sunday *New York Times*.

"So, Faith, how come Marlee is coming along?" Winnie asked, a bubble emerging from her chewing gum.

"Marlee's coming to look at the campus," Faith said. "Since she's a junior now, she's got to start thinking about college." She tried to concentrate on her little sister. But even after years of sharing the same house with Marlee, counseling and guiding her, Marlee's face wasn't clear.

"Remember being a high-school junior? Ah, those were the days." Winnie nudged Faith. "Does Marlee still idolize you?"

"She doesn't idolize me."

"Oh yeah? I remember that time we got our senior pictures taken," Winnie recalled, "and Marlee kept the really big one of you to put on her wall. Remember that, KC?"

KC lowered her paper and smiled. "Maybe she wanted to throw darts at it."

Faith tried to laugh.

"I never paid much attention to Marlee," KC said.

"You know, Faith, it's too bad your play is over," Winnie decided. "Your family would have been really proud to see the show you were assistant director of. Is that why you're bummed? Because your parents didn't come to see *Stop the World, I Want to Get Off?*"

"I'm not bummed!" Faith blurted as thoughts of Christopher Hammond filled every inch of her. All she could think of was his face, his hands, the smell of his aftershave, and the sound of his voice.

Winnie held up her hands. "I didn't mean to hit a sore spot."

"You didn't." Faith forced herself to think about something else. "I really am fine, but I'm a little concerned about what I'm going to do next."

"What do you mean?" KC asked.

Faith got up and began to pace. She forced herself to concentrate. "I found out that I have to think up an independent-study project."

"Why?"

"Since *Stop the World* closed before the semester was half over," Faith said, "I have to do something else if I want to get full class credit for being assistant director of the musical. And I have only two weeks to come up with an idea and write a proposal."

"You mean you can do anything you want and get credit for it?" Winnie's eyes got huge. "Can you study pizzamaking or rap music or the bizarre things freshmen do to decorate their dorm rooms?"

"Anything my advisor approves of, Winnie."

"So, Win, that probably nixes most of your ideas," KC cracked.

Winnie grinned and threw up her hands. "People always laugh at great creative minds."

"In the meantime," said Faith, "I'm going to help out at the campus day-care center three days a week. I start tomorrow. That was the only place my advisor could think of where I could fit in mid-semester. If I want, I can stay there through the winter, write a paper, and take a credit in early-childhood education."

"That sounds okay, Faith. You like kids. You were always the best babysitter of the three of us."

"KC's right," Winnie added. "The kids always liked you best. KC made them watch *Wall Street Week,* and I let them eat slugs."

Faith stood up. She paced to the soap dispenser and back, her boots slapping against the concrete floor. "I'll probably like the day-care center. I just wish I could keep doing something in the theater-arts department."

KC put her newspaper away. She focused her gray eyes on Faith. "So just think up a theater-arts independent study."

"It's not that easy," Faith countered, spinning back to look at KC. "I have to come up with a detailed proposal right away. My advisor says my project has to be realistic and well thought-out. I'm only a freshman. In two weeks I can't exactly organize my own production of *King Lear*. So maybe the day-care center is the best thing."

"Hey, why don't you ask Christopher for advice?" Winnie blurted. "He's a junior. He's big in the theater-arts department. Maybe he can help you organize something."

Hearing Christopher's name finally spoken out loud made Faith gasp.

"Winnie." KC grabbed Winnie's wrist and frowned. "Shhh!"

"I think it's a good idea," Winnie insisted. "Christopher might know exactly what to do. He knows everybody. What's wrong with asking him?"

"Winnie!"

Faith turned away. The tightness was turning

into something even more upsetting. It was almost hard to breathe.

One by one, the dryers stopped tumbling. For a moment all three girls stared at the floor in silence. Faith bolted over to the first dryer. She searched for change, but her hands wouldn't quite work. She fumbled. When she finally found a dime, she dropped it, then jammed it into the slot as if it didn't quite fit. The dryer didn't start right away, and she suddenly realized that she was pounding the dryer door.

Winnie and KC rushed over to join her.

"Faith!"

"Faith, you don't have to attack it. You just have to push the start button," said Winnie.

Faith collapsed against the dryer. "I don't know what I'm doing anymore."

"Faith, are you okay?" Winnie touched her shoulder.

"She'd be better if you could keep your mouth shut, Win." KC hugged Faith from the other side.

Faith wished that she'd never met Christopher, and at the same time, she couldn't imagine college without him. She ached when she hadn't seen him for a few days.

Faith had met Christopher during her first week at U of S, and had been his assistant director for his production of *Stop the World*. The show had been a great experience. It seemed like everything Christopher did was a rousing success. He was elegant and handsome and confident, an athlete and a fraternity bigwig. He was also a very talented theater director, so talented that he'd been chosen as an intern at the local TV station. But most important of all, he was also engaged to Suzanna Pennerman, a sorority princess at another college. At the same time, he was carrying on a very secret, very heavy romance with Faith.

"Winnie didn't think, Faith. Don't be upset."

"I'm not upset!"

"Anything new with Christopher?" Winnie ventured.

"Winnie," KC hissed, "shut up!"

"Nothing's new with Christopher." Trying to block out thoughts of him, Faith pushed the dryer's start button. She tried to mesmerize herself by watching the clothes as they flipped and twirled. "He says he wants to break off his engagement to Suzanna. I'm sure he will. Eventually."

"I guess," Winnie soothed.

"You'll figure it out," said KC.

"I'm just not sure what I'm supposed to do in the meantime," Faith finally blurted. Her body had begun to tremble. "I feel horrible always sneaking around. My parents and my sister think I'm so sweet and perfect. When I see them, I'll feel like a fake!"

"You don't have to tell them about Christopher," Winnie advised. "I've always been a big believer in not telling parents everything."

KC nodded.

The tightness inside Faith finally started to ease a little. She really looked at her two best friends, and took comfort from their familiar faces. "It's more than whether I tell them or not. I guess it's that I'm not the same person I was when we started school."

KC stared at Winnie, who stared back and then looked at Faith.

"None of us is the same," said KC. "All three of us have changed."

Faith didn't want to think anymore. She'd had enough of worrying and feeling guilty. She pushed herself away from Winnie and KC, stumbling back to her laundry bag and her books.

"Are you all right, Faith?" KC questioned.

"Faith?"

"I'm fine," Faith tried to convince herself.

"You're not acting fine." Winnie hugged her. "You know, Faith, it's okay not to be okay every once in a while—if you know what I mean."

"I told you both," Faith insisted, "I'm fine! Christopher is great. The day-care center will be great. I can't wait to see my folks."

"If everything's so hunky-dory with Christopher and you're going to be so happy to see your folks and Marlee," Winnie said, "how come you're crying?"

"I'm not crying," Faith gasped as she crumpled onto the bench again and heard sobs burst out of herself. She felt KC and Winnie put their arms around her as she took a deep breath and tears streamed down her face.

# Two

......................

*lick, click, click.*
    *Beep.*
    *Click, click, click, click, click.*

Lauren Turnbell-Smythe, Faith's roommate, stood in the office of the *U of S Weekly Journal* the next day, staring down at Dash Ramirez's ink-stained fingers. He was typing on the keyboard of one of the campus newspaper's computers and seemed to be going for a world speed record.

"You sure type fast for an assistant editor," she said.

Dash lifted his face, which was partially covered by two days' growth of beard. A bandanna held back his dark hair and a pencil was stuck in the corner of his mouth. "I can type this fast only when I'm writing something that doesn't take any brains —like this article about Parents' Visit and the Civil War football game. Pretty unimportant stuff. I can do this kind of piece in my sleep."

*Click, click, click, beep, click.*

Lauren watched Dash's fingers fly. She was a writer, but couldn't type nearly that fast. And Dash typed with only two fingers. "It's still impressive," she said. "Too bad there isn't an Olympic typing team."

Smiling, Dash reached across his desk, past empty coffee cups and crumpled food wrappers. He checked his notes. "You know, you're pretty witty for a sorority girl."

"I'm not a sorority girl."

"You're pledged to a sorority. Doesn't that make you a sorority girl?"

"Then I guess I'm an antisorority sorority girl."

Dash stopped typing and rubbed his chin. "Maybe that's what I should call this article. The anti–Parents' Visit Parents' Visit Story."

Lauren sat on the corner of Dash's desk and felt a little smug. Rich, shy, and chubby, she never would have imagined herself sitting in a university newspaper office, joking with a streetwise, sexy guy like Dash. Or if she had imagined it, she would have seen herself as tongue-tied and terrified. She would have been wearing the prim sorority suits her mother had picked out for her, and her shoulder-length hair would have been arranged in a wispy bob. Instead, her fair hair squiggled freely around her face. She wore a baggy sweater, parachute pants, and wire-rimmed glasses. There was even a new looseness to the waistband of her pants, making her suspect that over the last week she might have dropped a few pounds.

*Click, click, click, click. Beep.*

Dash leaned back and scrolled the text to the top of the computer screen. He took his pencil out of his mouth and balanced it on the edge of his desk. "Take a look at this. You're the creative-writing major. Tell me what you think."

"Well, you're the journalism major."

"That just means I know how to be obnoxious and bug people into telling me things they don't really want me to know. It doesn't mean I know how to write."

Lauren scanned the words on the screen. Dash's article was straightforward, explaining the events of Parents' Visit, which started that Thursday—special lectures for visiting parents, class visits, concerts, and meals—all culminating on Saturday in what was called the Civil War football game. It was the game between U of S and their rival from the southern corner of the state, the University of Evergreen.

The article even included the agenda for parents' events on Greek Row.

"It's fine," Lauren said. "It gives all the information."

"That's what I mean," Dash came back. "It's not exactly a Pulitzer Prize–winning subject. But sometimes even assistant editors have to pay their dues."

*Click, click, click, click.*

Lauren shrugged. "It's not like the article we wrote after our demonstration."

"That's for sure."

While Dash continued to type, Lauren watched the few other staffers lingering in the grungy office. Four or five reporters were having a conference in the back room. The advertising manager was arguing with someone over the phone, and the cartoonist was at her desk reading a comic book.

Still staring at the screen, Dash removed one hand from the keyboard and touched Lauren's wrist. He continued to type with one finger. "Did you see our piece in this week's issue?"

"Of course." Lauren blushed.

Together they'd written an article about Bickford Lane, a nearby row of houses owned by the university. The school had wanted to knock down the old houses to build a parking lot. Lauren and Dash had taken part in a risky demonstration against the parking-lot plan, and Lauren had even arranged for their protest to be covered by the local TV news. The result was that the university had backed down. Another result was that after a lifetime of pampered wealth and prissy private schools, Lauren had done something important and brave.

"Dash, are your mother and father coming to visit this week?"

Dash typed faster. "Actually, journalists don't have parents. We're born with ink on our fingers and cigars in our mouths."

"Dash. Are they coming?"

*Click, click, click, click.*

Lauren left Dash's nonanswer at that. As new and different as her life felt, she was still insecure Lauren Turnbell-Smythe, who had never had a boyfriend. She was still a little in awe of Dash and uncertain about their relationship. They qualified as just friends, because they'd never kissed. And yet there was a spark between them—at least there was a spark on Lauren's side. Lauren wondered if she were fooling herself by thinking there could ever be a spark on Dash's side as well.

She kicked her feet against Dash's desk. "My parents aren't coming. They're in Europe."

"Too bad." Dash reviewed his story and made a few corrections. "I wanted to meet them."

"Why?"

"I don't know if I've ever met super-rich people

before. I'd like to see them sitting through boring lectures and eating rubbery chili dogs in the student union, just like the rest of us peons."

"I wouldn't want to see it." Lauren slipped down off his desk. She hugged her middle and stood behind Dash's chair. "If my parents came to visit, the only place they'd want to see would be the Tri Beta sorority house. At least, that's all my mother would want to see. She doesn't care about my writing classes or the newspaper, or even my roommate or my dorm. She thinks sororities are the only reason to go to college."

"That's a novel approach to education."

"My mother also thinks that the only people worth knowing are the ones who belong to sororities and fraternities."

Dash stopped typing. He swiveled in his chair to look back at her. "So that's why you're in a sorority? Because of your mother?"

Lauren didn't want to admit that she'd been so wimpy as to let her mother bully her into rushing the Tri Betas, the top house on campus. The only reason the Tri Betas had accepted Lauren was because her mother had given them a large donation. "That's not the only reason," Lauren hedged.

Dash shrugged.

"Well, maybe it is the only reason. Anyway, I don't want to stay in the Tri Betas anymore. I certainly don't want to move out of my dorm and live in the Tri Beta house. My roommate, Faith, is much nicer than the sorority sisters. Actually, I've been trying to get myself kicked out."

"Really? Kicked out of the Tri Betas?"

Lauren nodded.

"What do you have to do? Use the wrong fork?" Dash leaned back in his chair, then propped his feet up on the corner of his desk.

"It's almost that ridiculous." Lauren stuck her hands in her pockets. "I didn't show up for required decorating sessions. I've been wearing the wrong kind of clothes."

He looked her up and down. "Tsk, tsk."

"Don't laugh. Those are big sins in Tri Beta land."

"I believe it."

"And I brought you to their homecoming party," Lauren admitted.

She waited for Dash's reaction. He'd gone with her to a homecoming reception at the Tri Beta house. It had hardly been a date, though. He'd wanted to go because he wanted background in case he ever wrote an exposé of the Greek system.

Dash smiled. "You brought me to that sorority party because you knew they'd hate me. I'm flattered."

"But they didn't hate you. They admired us both

for taking part in the Bickford Lane demonstration. They even thought you were . . ." She paused and cleared her throat. "Um, well, they thought you were sexy."

Dash's grin got even bigger. "Oh yeah? Like I said all along, sorority girls have great taste."

Lauren laughed. "So I still have to work on doing things wrong. I guess I'll have to sign up for more decorating sessions and then not show up. My parents may not be coming, but I'll still be required to go to all the events at the house during Parents' Visit. There's a parents' open house and parties at the fraternities after the football game. The Tri Beta sisters will want me to make paper flowers or sherbet punch or something equally important."

"Lauren, why don't you just quit? It's not a cult, is it? They haven't brainwashed you or anything."

Lauren felt like a wimp again. She didn't want to admit that her mother had threatened to stop giving her money if she quit the sorority. Lauren had hoped to avoid getting cut off by having the Tri Betas kick her out instead. "Um, it's just easier to get kicked out," she lied. "You know how sororities have all those weird traditions."

"Whatever you say. So you're going to keep trying to get out of sororityland?"

"I'm going to try as hard I can."

"Hey, wait a minute." Dash pitched forward over

his desk again and dropped the pencil out of his mouth. He stared at her over his shoulder. "Can you stay in the Tri Betas one week longer? It'll just be seven more days of paper flowers and using the right fork."

"Why?"

Dash lowered his voice and gestured for her to step closer. "I've always heard that the night of the Civil War football game is famous for some very raunchy fraternity hazing."

"Really?"

"I guess people get all worked up since it's the big game between the rival schools within the state. It's a notorious night for getting drunk and doing disgusting things."

"Lovely."

Dash nodded. "As soon as all the parents leave, frat guys always make some poor pledge drink a six-pack or two and then ride a motorcycle down Frat Row in his birthday suit. Or something sweet like that."

Lauren still wasn't sure what Dash was hinting at. "So?"

"So I've always wanted to get the real dirt on fraternity hazing. Everybody knows about the high points of the Greek system. The Interfraternity Council gives interviews about how wonderful they are all the time. But I've always wanted to write an exposé about the low points of that sacred institution."

"But hazing is illegal. Nobody's supposed to do stuff like that anymore."

"That's just the point," Dash stressed. "It's not supposed to go on anymore, but I've heard it still does. If I'm ever going to find out the truth, then I have to be able to see sorority and fraternity life from the inside." Dash looked down at his ink-stained jeans. "Believe it or not, none of the frat houses have invited me in. I'm not exactly the fraternity type."

"You want me to get you into some fraternity parties after the Civil War game?" Lauren realized. "Is that what you mean?"

Dash's dark eyes took in her whole face, making Lauren feel a little woozy.

He grinned and touched her cheek. "I always said you were smart."

*"Inhale one, two, three. Exhale one, two, three."*
Winnie bent over at the waist and let her head drop down to her knees. Her evening post-running stretch was something she looked forward to all day. Her limbs were loose and she had a great runner's high. In her Nike Air Stabs and purple Lycra unitard, Winnie could have challenged Florence

Griffith-Joyner for the most-flashily-dressed-runner award.

"Winnie, where do you get all your energy?" KC groaned. She was sprawled on the dorm green next to Winnie with her arms outstretched, looking as drained as if she'd just crossed the Sahara.

"I think devious thoughts." Winnie grinned and looked over toward Coleridge Hall, Faith and Lauren's creative-arts dorm. "KC, do you think Faith really had to study for her stagecraft class tonight? Or do you think she just didn't want to run with us?"

"It could have been either. Believe it or not, Win, people do study. And your runs are not always a bucket of fun."

"Sure they are. I just don't know how to read Faith sometimes. She seems okay and not okay at the same time. It's weird."

"Winnie, not everybody wears their heart on their sleeve."

"Like I do."

KC hugged her side. "But I also think Faith is really upset about Christopher and Parents' Visit," she said. "She started working at the day-care center today, and when I asked her how it went, she kept saying 'fine, fine, fine.' But you're right. Faith likes to act as if everything is super-wonderful when sometimes it's really not."

"So the day-care center is probably the total pits." Winnie did some deep lunges. "Well, personally, I think there's a chance for her and Christopher."

KC rolled her eyes. "Do you really?"

"Why not? Faith is pretty and smart and probably the most loyal, level-headed person I know. Why shouldn't Christopher be in love with her? Why shouldn't he dump Suzanna, as he keeps saying he's going to?"

KC stood up and brushed off her U of S sweats. "You sure sound like Pollyanna all of a sudden—especially considering your history with guys."

Winnie clutched her heart and staggered backward.

"Personally, I think it's dumb to get involved romantically with anyone your freshman year," KC lectured, getting a little carried away. "It's just a big distraction. We won't get ahead by wasting our energy on guys. We shouldn't even be thinking about guys or parents or any of this right now. We have more important things to do!"

*Important things like rushing a sorority with Lauren Turnbell-Smythe?* Winnie thought. When they had arrived at U of S, the Tri Betas were practically all KC had cared about. But for once Winnie kept her mouth shut. KC had been rejected by the Tri Beta sorority and gotten in a horrible feud with Lauren. Most recently, KC had broken off a romance with a rich guy named Steven Garth, who was in her business class.

"Maybe we do have more important things to worry about," Winnie couldn't resist saying. "But we are human, after all. I mean, KC, if your mom hadn't wasted her energy on your father, you wouldn't even be here right now."

KC ignored her. "I'd better go back to my dorm. I have to do a presentation tomorrow for my business-class discussion group. I don't want to blow this. I need to go over it a few more times." KC gave Winnie a quick hug, then marched off across the green.

"See you at breakfast," Winnie yelled.

Two boys playing Frisbee stopped their game to gawk at gorgeous KC, who looked right through them and kept on going.

"Cheer up. Remember nothing turns out as badly as you think it will," Winnie yelled again. "Except for the things that turn out worse." Winnie laughed at her own joke, and jogged off the other way, toward Forest Hall.

Dusk was turning to night and Winnie could barely make out the shape of her sterile-looking, brand-new dorm as she ran over the grass. There was no way not to hear it, however. Forest was a jock party dorm and, even though it was a Monday night, two or three stereos blasted at the same time.

As Winnie got closer, she could see people gathered in the lobby, lumped on sofas and sprawled on the floor. She heard laughter and hoots. She opened the lobby door and had to wonder if the Forest residents would clean up their act for Parents' Visit.

Winnie crossed the noisy lobby. Actually, she wasn't concerned about Parents' Visit. Her mom was pretty liberal. Divorced and a therapist, Mrs. Gottlieb was a big supporter of testing one's limits and doing one's own thing. She wouldn't be fazed by beer-can sculptures or guys and girls living in the same dorm.

Winnie dodged a squirt gun fight and made her way down the beige hallway to her room.

"What's this?" Winnie mumbled.

Usually half of Winnie's door was covered with absurd phrases cut out of newspapers and magazines, and on the other half of the door, a track schedule was posted for Winnie's roommate, Melissa McDormand. But that evening it looked like the entire door had been gift-wrapped. Reams of white computer paper were draped over and across the doorway.

As Winnie lifted some of the paper she began to suspect a prank by a rival dorm. She was wondering if she would find her entire room covered in computer paper, when she heard a happy male laugh and turned around.

"Hello?"

The voice was familiar and warm and the mere sound of it made Winnie feel bubbly. She looked around again but didn't see anyone.

"Hello there."

"Where are you?" Winnie questioned.

Josh Gaffey's head popped out of the tiny floor kitchen, which was only a few doors down. He smiled. "Yo."

The feeling inside Winnie turned even bubblier. This was like a runner's high multiplied by three.

Josh was munching on a bagel, and for a second Winnie just stared at him. Even though Josh lived right down the hall, she hadn't seen him for over a week. His dark hair looked a tiny bit longer than she remembered. His marbled blue earring was still there, along with his amused, friendly eyes and sparkling, happy smile.

"Looks like somebody did something weird and shocking to your door," he commented.

Winnie wanted to run, jump, and throw her arms around him. Instead she said, "Who do you think it could have been?"

Josh came out of the kitchen and leaned against the wall. He was barefoot and was wearing a T-shirt and what looked like his old high-school gym shorts. Wiry and tall, he was built like a swimmer. "Want a bite of bagel?"

Winnie slowly walked over to join him. She opened her mouth to take a bite, then took a step back. "How do I know the bagel's not booby-trapped?"

"Would I do something like that?"

"I don't know," she teased. "You're the same pervert who did shocking things to my door, aren't you?"

Josh gave the rest of his bagel to Winnie and slipped his arm through hers in one swift, totally natural move. Together, they walked back to her room. "It's the work of a maniac," he confirmed, tearing down globs of paper.

"A psycho."

"A frustrated techno-nerd computer major."

"Better notify dorm security." Winnie turned and smiled at him. Her whole body felt light.

He tousled her hair, then rearranged her spikes. They both laughed.

"So why did you do this?" Winnie asked.

"To get your attention. It worked, didn't it?"

"You could say that."

Josh kept smiling at her until Winnie had to look away from him. She couldn't believe how good it felt to be near him. Up until that point, their relationship had been very tangled, a series of misunderstandings and missed chances. During orientation Winnie had fallen for him instantly, then ruined it by drinking too much and passing out in his room. After that they'd become just friends, getting together on such a casual basis that Winnie hadn't known what to think.

"So how are you?" Josh asked.

"Good. Sweaty. I just ran."

Josh laughed and wrinkled his nose. "Essence de Winnie."

"I could bottle it and sell it as insect repellent." Winnie's eyes were glued to his. "How are you?"

"I've been chained to a computer for so long I'm growing silicon fingernails." Josh smiled. "I left that on your door because I'm sick of coming by when you're not here and leaving notes for you and not being sure if you even got them."

Winnie had gotten two notes from Josh. Both times he'd wanted to go out on the spur of the moment, when she'd already made plans to do something else. "I guess I just can't always be around when you decide to drop by at the last minute."

"Yeah. I hear what you're saying." He dug his hands in his pockets and thought for a minute. "So listen. My big computer project is over for the time being. I'm actually free to make plans. Should we make a date to get together this weekend?"

Winnie wanted to go out with Josh so badly she almost jumped up and down and screamed, *yes!* She didn't know what had changed things. Maybe it was because Josh had seen her on a date with someone else. Maybe creepy Matthew Kallender, a freshman Winnie had briefly dated and then dumped, had made Josh jealous.

"This weekend?" Winnie repeated. "My mother's coming all the way from Jacksonville. And I have homework." Winnie had worked hard to get caught up in her classes. She sensed that if she let her studies go, even Josh wouldn't make up for it. "I have a paper to finish for my history class. It's my first one and it's due next Monday."

"I forgot about Parents' Visit. My folks are coming for the football game on Saturday." Josh rocked on his heels. "So how about next Tuesday night? I know it's a class night, but we can celebrate your turning in your first paper. I don't know what we'll do, but I'll think of something." He smiled. "Or if you think of something first, we can do that."

Winnie wanted to jump for joy and throw her arms around his neck. Maybe KC and Faith were having a rough time lately, but she was beginning to think that freshman year was the best time ever. She smiled. "Okay."

"Yeah?" He clapped his hands and bounced up and down. "So, as they say, it's a date?"

She laughed. "It's a date."

Josh came toward her and for a moment everything went into slow motion. Winnie let her eyes close and remembered the first time he'd kissed her, how her legs had almost buckled and her heart had swelled with joy. She let her head fall back, felt Josh's hand on her shoulder and took a slow step closer.

But just then another girl burst out of the bathroom wearing a bathrobe and carrying a towel. She cleared her throat and Josh jumped back. He gave Winnie an embarrassed smile, bumped her shoulder with his, and started to walk back down the hall.

While Winnie stared after him, he said with mock seriousness, "By the way, Ms. Gottlieb, get that door cleaned up. It makes our whole floor look bad."

Giggling, Winnie tore off a streamer of computer paper and threw it at him.

# Three

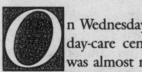

On Wednesday afternoon, Faith was at the day-care center for the second time. It was almost nap period, but the kids kept crawling around like mites on a plant.

*"Waaaaaaaaaaaaahhhhhhhhhh!"*

Five-year-old Lizzie Dunne had tripped over a wagon. She was wailing as if she'd been mortally wounded.

"Oh, Lizzie, don't cry. It'll be all right," Faith comforted, even though she had a deep ache of her own. Between the pressure of Parents' Visit, classes, the day-care center, and Christopher—whom she hadn't seen for four whole days—Faith wished that she could break down and cry, too. Nonetheless, she hugged Lizzie and patted her back.

"Come on, Liz."

Faith led Lizzie to the nap circle and thought about her second day at the Learning Tree. Along with two other U of S students, Chip Meyeroff and Shelley Lucci, Faith had spent the last hour supervising ten kids. She'd handed out juice and been barfed on by a little boy who had insisted on twirling in circles. Her heart felt as if it were cracking in two, but she still had a kind word and smile for everyone. Maybe she really was as nice as KC and Winnie thought she was.

"If you want graham crackers," Faith reminded the kids, "you have to sit down."

She waded through the toys and books. Two girls were trying to bonk each other on the head with rubber mallets. Faith intervened.

"Okay, everybody," Faith announced, "let's sit in a circle."

Chip and Shelley clapped their hands.

"Everybody settle down!" ordered Shelley.

"Okay, campers," cheered Chip, scooping up one child in each arm, "it's cracker-and-nap time."

"Is Faith going to read to us again?" asked a little boy named Jeremy.

Jeremy was a big fan of *Alice in Wonderland,* which Faith had read to them on Monday.

"Sorry. This time you'll have to put up with me," answered Chip.

The kids groaned and formed a lopsided circle. As Chip began reading a Dr. Seuss book, Faith picked up stray blocks and balls. Was this what college was supposed to be about? Her parents and Marlee were so excited about coming to see her that they were arriving that night, a whole day before Parents' Visit even began. Faith pictured herself avoiding the subject of Christopher, and then telling her family about her inspiring college experiences handing out graham crackers and picking up toys.

Carting a big box of children's books, Faith ordered herself not to think about it anymore. She went to the small storage room. Once she'd put everything away, she opened the back door, which led onto a small park. As soon as she looked outside, her heart revved up and her breath momentarily stopped. She was already out the door, not bothering to find out if they still needed her back in the day-care center.

"Christopher!" Faith cried.

There he was, leaning against the drinking fountain as if he were part of the landscape. Lean and auburn-haired, he was wearing a crisp blue shirt with the sleeves rolled up, dark slacks, and a striped tie. He looked like a handsome TV news anchor, and he had probably just come from his intern job at the TV station. Faith was stunned to see him, relieved and incredibly happy at the same time. Every time she saw him lately, she wondered if she would ever lay eyes on him again.

"Faith."

She ran across damp grass, through the hovering fog, weaving around a drinking fountain and the jungle gym until Christopher met her next to the swings. At once they were laughing and kissing and wrapping themselves in each other's arms. Hands touched hair and then faces, lips, arms. They flowed from strong hugs to light kisses, then into a slow, wonderful moment when they just looked into each other's eyes.

"What are you doing here?" Faith asked. It always seemed to be her first question, even though she knew the answer.

"Waiting for you." He grinned. "I haven't seen you for so long."

"Four days. Where have you been?"

He kissed her again. "You know how busy I get."

She looked away, trying not to think about Suzanna Pennerman. "I know."

"I just wanted to see you. I *had* to see you. I had to tell you something."

Faith reached for him again, and then all thought went out of her head. It all came down to touch—

soft hands, warm skin, and silky hair. His arms slipped around her waist—hers around his neck—and they were kissing, long, wonderful kisses right there in the middle of MacLaughlin Park.

They might not have stopped, except that Faith finally remembered the day-care center. "I've got to go back," she breathed.

Christopher nodded.

Still, neither of them took a step away. Lately Faith wanted to be so close to Christopher that it scared her. Every sober thought in her sensible head said that he was not the kind of guy for her. Sure, he was charming, successful and smart, but Faith couldn't forget that Christopher was also cheating on his fiancée. Worse, Christopher was never around when Faith really needed him.

"It's crazy always having to worry about who might see us," Faith admitted.

"I know." Christopher brushed back a wisp of her hair. "But maybe it won't be like this all the time."

"Really?"

He smiled and looked off at the line of birch trees that rimmed the park.

Faith rested her cheek against his shoulder. As exciting as all the secrecy was, it also hurt to be the girl on the side. Christopher showed up as if by magic whenever he felt like seeing her, but Faith never surprised him. Their relationship had unwritten rules, and one was that she never pop up at his track workout or the TV station. She'd never even been to ODT, his fraternity house, and other than their theater crowd, she'd never met any of his friends.

"How's it going at the day-care center?" Christopher asked.

"Fine, I guess." Faith took a deep breath. "How is everything with you?"

"Great. I've been planning the Civil War party for this weekend at the frat house. And working at the TV station." Christopher stepped back, loosened his tie, and looked up at the cloudy sky. "I think the station is going to let me direct a story for the news next month. All by myself."

"Really?" Faith drooped. Christopher's glittering success somehow made her feel more off balance. "I guess I wonder if I'm spinning my wheels here at the day-care center," she admitted. "If only I could think of a theater-arts independent study."

Christopher smiled his paper-white smile. "Maybe I can help you think of something."

"Would you do that? Oh, Christopher, that would be great."

"Sure." Christopher laughed. "Maybe we could recycle the set from *Stop the World*. Again."

"Maybe we could recycle the whole production

and use it as my independent study," Faith cracked. It had been her idea to reuse some old wooden boxes as a simple, nonrealistic set for *Stop the World*. The whole production had turned out to be a rousing success. She longed to work on another production and make it even more successful. "Or maybe we could work on another show together," Faith suggested. "Then at least we'd see each other more often."

Christopher nodded and looked into her eyes. He glanced around to make sure they were still alone and spoke more softly. "Faith, I talked to my friend Jamie, the guy I told you about."

"You did?" Faith's heart began to pump so fast that she felt unsteady.

"That's what I wanted to tell you." Christopher smiled. "Jamie's going to an athletic conference after the Civil War game. If we really want to be together, and not have to worry about other people, we could go up to his cabin next Wednesday night."

Jamie was a track buddy of Christopher's who lived in an isolated mountain cabin about ten miles out of town. Christopher had mentioned going up to the cabin before. Nothing had been spelled out, but Faith knew what going would mean. What she didn't know was how that would change their relationship. Their relationship certainly needed to change. She needed to know that Christopher would be there when she needed him.

"What do you think?" Christopher whispered, pulling her close again.

Faith was unable to think.

"I think it would be great not to worry every two seconds about being found out," Christopher added. "We could really be alone."

The idea of being alone with Christopher made Faith feel dizzy. But a moment later, the painful tightness came back. She imagined not seeing Christopher at all until Sunday, not even exchanging a hello, and then going to the cabin. Their relationship was all stolen embraces and secret looks, especially since *Stop the World* had closed. Faith yearned for a little ordinary time when they could just be themselves.

"Faith," Christopher persisted, "what do you think?"

Faith also wondered if Suzanna would visit that weekend. Parents' Visit and the Civil War game were big social events on Frat Row. Would Suzanna be Christopher's public date, escorting him to the Saturday night frat party and the game, while Faith waited to be whisked away secretly to an isolated mountain retreat?

Christopher touched Faith's chin, making her tip her face up to look at him. "What's the matter?"

Faith wanted to tell him a hundred different things. *I don't trust you. I may be in love with you, but I'm scared. If I take such a big step and go to the cabin with you, what kind of commitment will I get from you in return?*

"What about Suzanna?" she finally mumbled.

"Faith, forget about Suzanna," Christopher promised. "Suzanna and I will be over soon. It's just you and me. You're the one that matters. We should go to Jamie's cabin and be together."

"You're right," Faith finally whispered, and then she was in his arms again.

KC was in the middle of her business-class presentation that same afternoon when she caught the eye of her partner and former boyfriend, Steven Garth. His handsome face no longer mocked her. He didn't shake his Rolex watch, flip a loafer with his bare foot, or lounge in his desk chair as if he were tanning on an exclusive beach. Instead he sat pitched over his desk, wearing a pastel polo shirt, listening to her speech with apologetic eyes and a mouth that seemed to have used up its clever smiles.

"To sum up the project that we completed last week," KC lectured, using every bit of concentration to keep herself on track, "our group formed a partnership called Soccer, Inc." She held herself stiffly at the lectern, wearing high heels, a blazer, and a knife-pleated skirt.

Steven nodded as if he were actually offering moral support.

KC didn't trust his warm looks. She checked her notes and continued to speak. "We bought soccer shirts from Bernhard's Wholesale Athletic Supply in downtown Springfield and resold them to the members of the intramural soccer teams."

Steven was still listening intently, making KC wonder whether he was getting ready to somehow embarrass her. When they had dated, Steven had always had an insult ready. KC had broken up with him after he'd even put her down in front of his rich father.

Clearing her throat, KC went on with her speech. "Our experience has taught the partners of Soccer, Inc. a great deal about supply and demand, marketing, accounting, and salesmanship."

KC still couldn't believe that she'd opened up to Steven before figuring out that he was only interested in pulling rank on her. He'd only wanted to remind her that she wasn't from a rich, powerful business family. He'd wanted her to remember that even though she'd learned to be savvy and ambitious, she would never measure up to someone who'd been born into wealth.

Tapping her papers against the lectern, KC read

her final note. "And we turned a profit of five dollars per shirt in the process."

There was applause from the class. KC smiled and put her notes back in her briefcase. She was about to ask for questions when Steven slowly stood up.

"I'd like to make one other point," Steven interjected before KC could stop him. There was a new softness in his voice. "I would like to make a proposal for myself and my partners of Soccer, Inc. I've okayed this with two of my partners already, and I'm sure my fourth partner will agree with us." He smiled at KC. "Since our business was intended as a class project, rather than a money-making venture, we've decided to donate all of our profit to the U of S Food Bank."

"What?" KC whispered.

Some class members frowned, but most applauded. Naomi, the teaching assistant, nodded in appreciation. Helen and Edward, the other two partners in Soccer, Inc., cheered with approval. Steven rested his eyes on KC, as if he actually expected her to jump up and applaud, too.

KC was stunned! How dare Steven surprise her like that? Not that she was against donating money to charity, but she'd always assumed that she would keep her share of the profit. Steven didn't have to worry about paying for clothes and blue books. But she'd even had to steal money from the Soccer, Inc.

account to pay her bills. She'd finally paid Soccer, Inc. back, then quit her part-time job delivering the dorm mail, but all that had left her flat broke. How could he do this to her?

"Thank you, Steven," KC managed. She had no choice but to hide her rage. She had to keep up a businesslike appearance, even though she was afraid she might start screaming. "That's the end of my presentation." Hoping that her grade wouldn't suffer from such an abrupt ending, she collected her papers, and staggered back to her seat.

Other students made presentations as the class period went on, but KC barely took in a word. All she was aware of was Steven's sad stare and the fury heating up inside her. By the time the class was over, her heart was racing. She held her briefcase so tensely that her knuckles were white.

Steven caught up with her after she had pushed her way out the doors into the heavy, damp air. He raced her down the outside stairs, cutting in front of her and almost making her trip. "What is it, KC?" he demanded. "Don't be mad. I didn't do it to make you mad."

"We have nothing more to say to each other," KC spat out. "I would like to concentrate on my work and not have you distracting me in the middle of my presentations. And if you call me 'partner,' or

'Little Angel,' or any of the other stupid names you used to call me, I will laugh in your face."

"I have no intention of calling you any of those names anymore, KC," he said softly. Everything about him seemed softer and sadder. "I know I made some mistakes with you. I made one big mistake when I acted like such a jerk with my dad. Okay, I admit it, I'm a jerk sometimes. But I didn't do it to put you down. I did it because my dad was putting *me* down."

"That's your problem." KC walked faster. It was cold and she had begun to shiver. "That's between you and your father, Garth. It has nothing to do with me anymore."

"Yes, it does," he argued, sticking by her side. His eyes never left her. "Come on, KC. We need to talk about this. I can't believe you can be so cut off from me now. I'm not asking for our old relationship. I know I blew that. But we have a lot in common. Even you have to admit that. How about just being friends?"

"Friends?" KC scoffed. "A friend wouldn't have done what you just did to me."

He stood in front of her and tried to grab her arms. "Are you against giving money to hungry people? They need it, KC. I thought you'd be the first person to admit that."

She wrenched herself away. "I need the money, too, Garth."

"You can always borrow money from me."

"I'd rather flunk out."

"Don't be so melodramatic, KC."

"I'm not being melodramatic. I'm being realistic." She held back tears. She'd cried once in front of Steven. There was no way she was going to let him see her cry again. She walked faster, down a bicycle path and through the fog. "You say you want to be friends. Believe me, I don't need friends like you."

"Everybody needs friends, KC. Even friends like me."

"I don't."

He finally stopped pursuing her. He stood back and shook his head. "When you act like this I wonder if you're really alive. It's not fair."

KC stopped and faced him. There was a vulnerability in his face that got to her. She still remembered kissing him, but she forced herself to push those images out of her head. "Oh, and you're so fair? Is that why you gave my money away without even asking me? Because you're so fair?"

Steven grabbed her shoulders. "Will you listen to me? I did it to apologize to you, KC. I did it to prove that I'm not just a spoiled rich kid. I thought you might like that. You think you're so superior to me just because I have money and your parents are so pure and free. I thought it might impress you because it's something your hippie parents might have done."

Steven was right. It was exactly something KC's flakey parents would have done. "Oh come on, Garth! You did it to get back at me. You did it to put me down."

"I never have put you down, KC. And I never will."

A tiny part of KC softened. Something inside her wanted to give in, to wrap herself in Steven's arms, weep on his shoulder, and start all over again. But she couldn't do that. She had to stop these feelings before they got her in trouble. If she hadn't fallen for Steven in the first place, her whole freshman fall would have been so much easier. She coldly wrenched herself away from him.

KC pushed past students rushing to class and took a detour down a steep, grassy bank. When she was sure that Steven was no longer following her, she ducked into a phone booth behind the library and began furiously punching numbers.

"You think I'm so superior to you, Steven," she muttered sarcastically. "Ha ha. You want to be my friend. What a joke. And you think that my parents are so pure and free. Give me a break, Steven. You know my parents are fools. Why don't you just come right out and say it? Pretty soon they'll come and visit and everyone else will know it, too."

The operator came on. "May I help you?"

"Collect call to anyone at the Windchime Restaurant, from Kahia Cayanne," KC said, pulling the door tightly shut.

"One moment please."

"Come on," KC ranted as the phone rang and rang and rang. "Answer the phone! Someone has to be in the kitchen."

Finally, KC's father picked up. "Windchime Natural Foods Restaurant," he greeted in a laid-back voice. Classical music blasted in the background. When the operator tried to ask him if he would accept the call he said, "I can barely hear you. Hold on and let me turn the music down."

No wonder her parents never made any money, KC thought. If she were calling with a big dinner reservation, she would have hung up by now!

Her father came back on the line. He accepted KC's call. "Kahia! Hi, hon. I was just thinking about how much I miss you. What's up?"

KC started talking. "Dad, are you still planning to come for Parents' Visit?"

"Wouldn't miss it for the world," he said. "I guess Faith's folks are getting there tonight, before the official start. I'm afraid I'll be a day late. I need to be here and get everything prepped. But your mom and Miranda decided that they can handle the weekend by themselves, so I can be there Friday night."

KC wanted to scream. She pictured her father strolling around campus with his long, thinning hair, wearing one of those ridiculous embroidered shirts. She could just imagine running into the girls from the Tri Beta sorority. "Are you sure that's a good idea, Dad? If you come here, only one person will be in the kitchen all weekend."

He laughed. "What's more important, Kahia? Some dinners or my daughter? Besides, your sister can work the floor and help out your mom at the same time. If Miranda gets behind, customers will just have to wait."

KC cringed. "Dad, I don't think you should leave Mom and Miranda alone."

He paused. "Well, I guess we could close up for the weekend. Then we all could come to visit you."

KC felt sick. "You can't just close up, Dad! That would be terrible for business." She took a deep breath. "Actually, I've got a lot of homework to do this weekend, too. I really don't need distractions right now. Maybe we should see each other another time."

"Whoa, Kahia, what's going on here? We haven't seen you since you left for school. Is there something wrong?"

"Nothing's wrong." KC swallowed hard. She felt

as if she were closing off her heart for the second time that day. "Dad, I don't want you to come."

"What?"

"Don't come to visit, Dad. I don't want to see you."

There was a very long pause. Finally her father said in a low, hurt voice, "Okay. I'm not sure what I did to make you say something like that. But if you don't want me to come, I won't."

The telephone went dead as KC felt another little piece of her heart ice up.

# Four

......................

**A**fter leaving the day-care center that afternoon, Faith had wandered around campus, convinced that she was the most sophisticated of college freshmen. After all, she was having an intense romance with one of the most desirable men on campus. The more she thought of sneaking away to meet him at Jamie's cabin, the more grown-up and heady she felt.

Then she'd found her parents and Marlee waiting for her at the dorm and her feelings had flip-flopped. She didn't want to think about Christopher and Jamie's cabin. How could she possibly explain to her parents what she was about to do? The two parts of her life didn't fit together, and it made her feel like an inexperienced kid again.

"I'm glad you came a day early," Faith said to her parents and Marlee as she held out her plate for overcooked spaghetti and watery sauce. They were eating dinner in the dining commons, joined by Winnie, KC, and Lauren. "You get to see dorm food as it really is."

"It's like being an undercover eater," Winnie cracked. "By the time the rest of the parents get here tomorrow, they'll have cleaned the place up. The serving ladies won't be wearing their hairnets and they'll be serving prime rib."

"Winnie's right," said KC. "And as soon as you all leave, we'll be back to bread and water again."

Lauren stared at her tray and didn't say anything.

Faith laughed. Her parents were still in their traveling clothes and looked out of place against the sloppy students in their sweats and torn jeans grabbing extra rolls. Marlee didn't fit in either. She was a duskier, frailer version of Faith, wearing a sloppy black jacket decorated with the logo of some rock band Faith had never heard of. Even though it was almost dark outside, Marlee wore sunglasses. She looked so different from how Faith remembered her, like a moody high-school student trying hard to appear sophisticated.

"I think there's a big table way in back," Faith

said. Suddenly she felt as unsure of herself as Marlee seemed to be. How could she feel sure when half of her wanted to be the nice, old Faith, the predictable daughter who got good grades and dated the nicest guy in town? Meanwhile, the other half of her was a grown-up woman who was fully prepared to spend the night with a guy who was engaged to someone else.

"We're following you, honey," said Faith's father.

"You lead the way," said her mom.

"Okay." In her old cheerleading voice, Faith led everyone farther into the dining room. "Let's go."

KC, Winnie, and Lauren made their way out of the serving area. Faith's mother and father followed, too, but Marlee hung back, holding a nearly empty tray and blocking traffic.

"Come on, Marlee," Dr. Crowley urged in a sweet, overly patient-sounding voice.

"I'm the only high-school student here," Marlee grumbled. "I told you I would be."

Faith's mother and father exchanged big smiles.

"No you're not," said Mrs. Crowley.

"What does it matter, Marlee?" said Faith's dad.

"Just wait until my mother gets here tomorrow," Winnie joked, guiding Marlee away from the serving area. "The way my mom dresses, everyone will think she's in high school, too."

Marlee followed Faith through the noisy dining room.

"Marlee," Faith said when they all reached a long table in back, "I don't care if you are the only high-school junior here. I'm glad you came." She hoped she hadn't sounded like a sickeningly sweet phony, and tried to pat Marlee's shoulder, the way she'd done a thousand times back home. But Marlee scooted past Faith and sat down.

Faith wasn't sure what to make of her sister's sudden grumpiness. When Faith had been at home, Marlee had always seemed as breezy and uncomplicated as the rest of the family. She'd worn jumpers and faded sneakers, talked on the phone, played volleyball, and read books. Faith told herself that it was probably just some trendy teenage phase. A lot had certainly changed in her own life recently. She felt like she was leading a double life. Maybe Marlee had changed as well.

They all hovered around the table, not sure where to sit.

KC finally put down her tray, then realized that Lauren was plopping down in the chair next to her. KC popped up again. "Excuse me," KC snapped, glaring at Lauren and moving to the other side of the table. "I'll sit here."

"Excuse *me.*" Lauren was on her feet, ready to

move, too. When Winnie replaced KC, she finally sat down again.

Faith remembered the feud between KC and Lauren and realized that she never should have asked them to eat at the same table. She wondered if her parents and Marlee had noticed the testy exchange between her roommate and KC. She hoped not. All she wanted was to get through Parents' Visit with pleasantness and no problems.

"Did everybody get what they needed?" Faith asked, trying to cover her own discomfort.

"This looks great," cheered her dad as he looked down at his tray.

"I think this spaghetti really looks delicious," agreed her mother.

"Don't bet the farm on it," joked Winnie. "But it's better than the tuna surprise." Winnie stuck out her tongue. "Now that is a surprise, believe me."

Everyone laughed.

"Let's eat," Faith said, feeling almost like she was at the day-care center again.

They chowed down in silence while Faith stared at her folks. Her parents looked eerily the same, as if not one minute had passed since she'd last seen them. Her mom's short hair was tightly curled. She wore a belted shirtdress and a little pearl pin, while her dad looked neat in his blazer and tie.

"I ran into one of your old high-school teachers,"

Faith's dad mentioned. "Mr. Hanson. His dog got cut up in some barbed wire, and Mr. Hanson brought him into my office to be patched up. He said to tell the three of you hello."

"That's nice." Faith looked from KC to Winnie. She wondered if they were thinking the same thing she was—that high school and Mr. Hanson's government class seemed like a whole different lifetime.

Her father laughed. "Mr. Hanson reminded us of the time your class was supposed to interview someone in the Jacksonville city government. His version of it was that Winnie was supposed to talk to the parks commissioner, but never made it to the interview."

Winnie put her hands to her face. "One of my many high school disasters."

Dr. Crowley wagged a finger at her. "Winnie, Mr. Hanson said you rode downtown with some kid on a motorcycle and never even made it back to school that day."

"All true." Winnie giggled with embarrassment. "Mr. Motorcycle's name was Greg Talisman. He was actually kind of a major creep. I blew my government grade because of him, and the next week he dumped me."

Dr. Crowley clucked his disapproval. "I've always told Faith and KC to teach you to use better judgment, Winnie. I hope they're still doing that."

"Actually," Winnie smiled, "I'm into good judgment myself these days. I've had enough Greg Talismans to last me until I'm twenty-one."

Faith's father pointed to KC. "KC, Mr. Hanson told us that you wrote the head of the city planning committee such a good letter that she couldn't wait to talk to you. When she finally met you, she was very impressed."

KC played with her food. "I remember. But I don't think she was all that impressed with me."

"And you, Faith," Mrs. Crowley said, looking at her daughter. "Mr. Hanson told us what you did for that assignment too."

"What did he say?" Faith was trying to remember the role she'd played in that government assignment when she got an odd flash of déjà vu. Out of the corner of her eyes she'd seen a glimpse of blond ringlets. When she looked up, her heart flipped. She hoped it was Christopher, finally greeting her in a public place. She wanted to jump up and embrace him, even in front of her parents.

But it wasn't Christopher.

Faith took in the outdoorsy guy in hiking shorts and a red parka. She stared at his face and thought she was back home in Jacksonville, sitting around her parents' kitchen table after high-school soccer practice. It was Brooks Baldwin, her former boyfriend, who was also a freshman at U of S.

"Brooks!" said Faith's mother.

"Dr. and Mrs. Crowley," Brooks said with terrific grace. He set down his dinner tray, shook hands with Faith's dad, then kissed her mom on the cheek.

"How wonderful to see you," said Faith's father. "I was hoping we'd run into you."

"Sit down," Faith's mom invited, pulling out a chair. "Join us for dinner."

"How are you?"

"Fine, Dr. Crowley. Just fine." Brooks flashed a brief look at Faith. For one quick moment their eyes locked, then Brooks sat in a chair next to Marlee.

"It's good to see you again, Dr. and Mrs. Crowley," Brooks said, looking away from Faith. "I just wanted to say a quick hello."

"Are your dad and stepmom coming?" asked Faith's mother. Her tone was as friendly as it had been when Brooks and Faith had still been a couple.

Brooks nodded. "They're coming tomorrow."

Faith suddenly wanted to be anywhere but at that table. In high school, she'd assumed that she and Brooks would never split up. But she'd suddenly broken up with Brooks during freshman orientation, after realizing that they'd been on the rocks for a long time. Brooks had avoided her ever since.

"I was just talking about that time you all were

supposed to interview someone in Jacksonville government for Mr. Hanson's class back home," Dr. Crowley reminded Brooks.

Brooks glanced at Faith again. His eyes looked sad and his mouth tightened.

That was when Faith remembered her part in that high school interview assignment. She'd worked on the assignment with Brooks, of course. In high school, she'd shared everything with Brooks. Together, they'd spoken to someone on the Jacksonville city council. The man had been so impressed with Brooks that he'd invited him to talk to the mayor, too. Brooks had insisted that Faith go back again with him and interview the head of the arts council. And of course, through no choice of her own, Faith had gone.

Faith sank down in her chair. She used to smile and let Brooks do a lot of things for her. One of the reasons she'd broken up with him was to confront college and make choices on her own.

"The food's getting cold," Faith reminded everyone, after an uncomfortable pause.

They all turned their attention back to dinner and chattered about safe subjects, such as Brooks' intramural soccer team and the arrival of Winnie's mom.

"How about your dad?" Dr. Crowley asked KC.

KC paled. "My dad decided not to come," she

said in a funny voice. "Uh, he couldn't get away. You know how busy weekends can be at the restaurant."

"That's odd," bantered Faith's mom. "Your dad told me he wouldn't miss this visit for anything."

KC played with her spaghetti, then pushed her plate away. "Well, he changed his mind. He realized that his business is much more important than this silly Parents' Visit."

Dr. and Mrs. Crowley exchanged glances. After that, they all ate in silence. Faith and her parents smiled, while Lauren, KC, Brooks, and Marlee stared down at their plates and tried not to acknowledge the silent tensions crisscrossing the dinner table.

As soon as everyone finished eating, Winnie jumped up. "Let's all go on a campus tour," she suggested. "I can show you all the bizarre places— the running path around the old pioneer graveyard, and the place on the statue near the student union where everyone sticks their used chewing gum. Lauren can show you the newspaper office. KC can take you to the business school, and Faith can take you around the theater." She clapped her hands, making her bracelets rattle. "How about it?"

"I don't know," KC hedged, picking up her tray and glancing at Lauren again.

"I have to go over to Sorority Row," Lauren reacted, backing away from the table. "I have to help decorate the Tri Beta living room for the parents' open house." She picked up her tray. "Bye, Dr. and Mrs. Crowley. Nice to meet you."

"You, too, Lauren."

"I hope we see more of you."

Lauren disappeared into the dining hall crowd and KC relaxed. "Maybe Winnie has the right idea. Let's go on a campus tour."

They bussed their trays, but before they could all collect outside, KC, Winnie, and Marlee detoured back to the dessert counter to grab a few chocolate-chip cookies. Meanwhile Faith, Brooks, and Faith's parents went out the back door to wait for them.

As soon as they stepped out into the damp fall air, Faith's mother shivered. She took her husband's hand. "Honey, let's run to the Jeep and get our sweaters. It's getting so cold and foggy."

Faith glanced over at Brooks and shivered, too. "I'll loan you one of mine, Mom," she blurted. "We can just stop by my room."

But her parents were already walking toward the dorm parking lot, and Faith was alone with Brooks. She couldn't help wondering if her folks had left them alone intentionally, hoping that she and Brooks would get back together.

For a moment they both stood very still. Faith sat down on the low concrete retaining wall and looked off at the fog that hovered over the campus, completely hiding the mountains.

Soon Brooks sat a few feet away from her, kicking his boots against the retaining wall and staring at the ground.

"Are you cold?" he asked.

"Oh no." Faith hugged her bare arms, hiding goosebumps. "You don't have to wait with me. I don't mind waiting alone."

"I haven't seen you for a while." Brooks blew on his hands. "Not even in the dining commons."

Faith prayed that Winnie, KC, and Marlee would get their dessert and hurry up. "I was really busy with *Stop the World*. I got a lot of sandwiches to go and even missed a bunch of meals. It was a great experience."

"I bet it was." Brooks looked away. "I guess Christopher took up a lot of your time."

Faith couldn't ignore the resentment in his voice. "What?"

"You said you broke up with me because you wanted to find yourself. And then the first thing you did was hook up with Christopher Hammond, a guy who's engaged to somebody else. That's all."

Faith was overtaken once again by the terrible, tight feeling in her chest.

"Are you still seeing him?" Brooks demanded.

Faith shrugged. Brooks had somehow known

about her and Christopher almost before she and Christopher had even gotten together.

"That means yes."

"I didn't say that."

"Maybe not. But I know it's true. Doesn't it bother you that he has a fiancée?"

Faith knew that Brooks would never dream of getting involved with a girl while he was engaged to somebody else. So he didn't understand what was going on with her and Christopher. How could he, when she didn't understand it herself? "Why does it matter to you?"

Brooks jumped down off the wall. His handsome face looked angry and hard. "I'm just trying to put it all together, Faith."

"Put what together?"

"You. What happened to us. I thought I knew you so well, but now I think you've changed into a totally different person."

"I'm the same person," she argued. "It's just college that's different."

"Right. You're the same Faith, and you think it's okay to see a guy in secret when he's going with another girl?"

"I . . . I don't know. You don't know either!" she stammered. She wondered what Brooks would think if he knew about her going with Christopher to Jamie's cabin. "Maybe I am a different person. Maybe I should be different."

"Not different in that way." Brooks backed away and shook his head. "I don't know you any more, that's for sure."

He started to leave, then turned back. "I've been a real fool, Faith. I thought I really missed you, but there's no one to miss because the Faith I was in love with doesn't exist anymore."

Faith watched him walk away. By the time Brooks had passed the commons and started jogging across the green, she didn't recognize him anymore either.

# Five

"Conflict simmered until a full state of war erupted among the ancient Greek city-states," Dr. Hermann lectured.

"Western civ," KC printed in big letters across the top of her note paper. "Conflict." Conflict seemed to be an apt word to describe her life lately. Between Steven, her father, and Lauren, KC felt like *she* were about to shut down after an unending state of siege.

KC shifted. Parents were visiting the class that Thursday, so every seat was filled, plus there were some people sitting in folding chairs and others leaning against the wall. KC felt squeezed in. Since she'd arrived at the last minute, she'd been forced to sit between Lauren and Winnie's mother, who'd arrived that morning. Mrs. Gottlieb was friendly and interested, but being so close to Lauren felt like being shoved against a barbed wire fence.

KC tried to listen to the lecture, writing down everything that could get into her distracted brain, until she caught Faith's eye. Faith was a few rows down with her folks and she looked distracted, too.

KC suspected that neither she nor Faith was really paying attention. Hermann's conflict lecture just kept making KC think about her father. How she'd gone crazy with her first credit card and had taken money from Soccer, Inc. to pay off the charges; how hard she'd had to work to make up the Soccer, Inc. money; and how she hadn't been able to deal with Steven after he'd found out what she had done. And now he wanted to be friends.

KC glanced at Lauren. During orientation week, KC and Lauren had been friends. They had rushed the Tri Beta sorority together. They both would have been accepted, but KC had stood up for Lauren after a cruel rush prank, and that had destroyed her chances of getting in. Then, when KC had asked Lauren for the simplest favor—a loan to pay back Soccer, Inc.—Lauren had refused to help her in return.

KC's cold anger was disrupted by a smattering of applause from parents as Dr. Hermann snapped up his map of the warring ancient world and took an embarrassed little bow. The lecture was over. Students were leading their folks up the aisle and checking their Parents' Visit schedules.

KC made her way out to the busy hall. Faith's parents and Marlee waved as they headed toward a theater-arts department presentation with Faith. Winnie's mother was chatting with other visitors, while Winnie tugged at KC.

"My mom and I are going off campus for lunch," Winnie told KC. "She's taking me to a sushi bar. Do you want to come?"

KC shook her head. "No thanks, Win."

"Are you sure?"

KC couldn't imagine enjoying lunch with Winnie and her mom. "Isn't sushi raw fish?"

Winnie wrinkled up her nose. "I've never had it either. But you know my mom. She thinks it's always good to be adventurous."

"Thanks, Win, but I'm not up to it right now."

Winnie leaned toward KC and whispered, "Why don't you come anyway? Then if I chicken out, I can hide my sushi under your napkin."

"No," KC said. The classroom doors were closing again and the hallway was thinning out. "I'd better go over my lecture notes while I can still remember a few things. Midterms are coming up. I don't want to get behind."

"I know how that is." Winnie noticed her mother waiting for her at the other end of the hall. She jogged down to meet her and called back to KC, "We'll all meet for dinner tonight! If I'm still alive."

"Okay. See you tonight."

Alone, KC stood against the wall, staring at the smudged linoleum floor, the fluorescent lights, and the cluttered bulletin boards. The next class period had just started, and she could hear a woman launch into a lecture on the economic factors behind the American Revolutionary War. KC clutched her briefcase and began to walk, listening to her high heels clomp and clack down the corridor. There was no one else in the hall until KC passed the ladies' room. Then the door swung open and out walked Lauren.

"Oh," said Lauren.

KC didn't say a thing.

They strode side by side. At first they couldn't help glancing at each other, but then they both stared straight ahead again, as if in military formation. They marched like two robots, out the double doors, into the cold air, and alongside a bicycle path. It was clear that they were both headed back to the dorms. By the time they'd passed the University Theater and Mill Pond, the silence had become so ridiculous that one of them had to say something.

"Are you going to your sorority house tonight?" KC asked icily. She knew that Parents' Visit and the Civil War football game were big deals on Sorority Row.

"Actually I'm not," Lauren barked back. "I have to be there tomorrow. Tonight I'm meeting my friend Dash Ramirez at a meeting of the Progressive Students' Coalition. We're working on a publicity campaign to help the U of S Food Bank."

The last thing KC wanted to hear about was the U of S Food Bank. "Good for you."

"Don't say something you don't mean." Lauren's voice had a forcefulness that KC had never heard before. Even her pale, round face looked harder and more determined. They walked around the old pioneer graveyard and past the new computer center.

"What?"

"I'm sure you don't wish anything good toward the Progressive Students' Coalition," Lauren explained. "I'm sure you'd like nothing better than to see the coalition be completely destroyed."

"That's not true."

Lauren ignored her. "But that isn't going to happen. Ever since we got the regents to back down about tearing down those houses on Bickford Lane, the coalition has been stronger than ever. No thanks to you."

KC knew what Lauren was referring to. KC had

found out about the coalition's secret demonstration plans and tipped off the police. She'd told herself that she'd ratted because she feared the demonstration might get violent. And yet KC knew she'd really done it out of pure spite.

Avoiding a touch football game, they crossed the dorm green. KC's body moved as if on automatic pilot. She was so angry and confused that she could barely think.

"Do you know what I think about you?" Lauren said accusingly.

"No."

"I think you like to destroy things. Including people's feelings."

KC was beginning to feel faint. She flashed on Steven's feelings. Lauren's feelings. Her father's feelings.

They'd come to a fork in the paths that crisscrossed the green. Lauren took off her glasses and wiped them with the hem of her sweater. Her eyes were an astonishing violet color. "Do you remember the last thing you said to me? Before today, I mean."

"No." KC had been trying hard not to remember much about what had gone on between her and Lauren.

"Well, I remember, KC." Lauren put her glasses back on. The glasses made her face look purposeful and smart. "I asked you why you'd ratted on us, and you told me you didn't know. You said you didn't know why you did a lot of things. All I can say, KC, is that you have been doing things that are spiteful and mean. And if you don't know why you're doing them, you'd better find out."

Cool jazz hummed. Glasses clinked. Winnie and her mother sat on tippy stools, facing a sushi bar done in stark black and white tiles.

"Mom, you just got to Springfield. How did you find out about this great place already?"

With her wild, curly hair, long earrings, and flowing, layered clothes, Winnie's mom looked more like a sculpture student than a small-town therapist. "Winnie, you've been here all fall," she answered. "How could you *not* have found out about this great place?"

Winnie laughed. "It's great to see you, Mom."

"You too, Win. I've missed you."

"I've missed you too. You're the only person I know who makes me look conservative." Winnie tasted a chunk of raw tuna, then looked up in surprise. "Hey, this is good! Even better than tuna surprise."

"Of course it's good." Her mother tossed her long earrings, then dropped a squiggle of ginger on

Winnie's plate. "It's wonderful. I can't believe you haven't tried sushi before."

"Yeah, well, believe it or not, there's a few things at college I haven't tried yet."

Her mother put down her chopsticks and looked at Winnie, curious but not concerned. "So, how is it? How are you? Tell me everything, Win. Although I have to say, I can tell by the way you look that you're doing well."

"I am." Winnie ran a hand through her spiky hair. "I really am. Sometimes I can't believe it. I keep waiting for the bogeyman to jump out of my closet and tell me I'm going to mess up again."

"Why should you mess up again, Win? You've learned from your mistakes, haven't you? That's what mistakes are for."

"I know." Winnie wished that she hadn't had to make so many mistakes. As much as she adored her mom, she wouldn't have minded a few warnings ahead of time. "At least now I'll know to send my dorm deposit in on time next year." She rolled her eyes, remembering the first day of orientation, when she'd found out they'd given her original room to someone else. "And I know how to get along with my roommate."

"Melissa?"

"Yeah. I like her. I don't see her that often since I

mostly hang out with Faith and KC. Melissa's pre-med and running track."

"Sounds like a real overachiever."

"Yeah. Especially compared to me."

Winnie's mom patted her hand across the table. "Winnie, don't worry. You're very bright. You'll figure out what you want to do."

"Yeah." Winnie shrugged. "Believe it or not, I like my History of Russia class and Western Civ. Even French is okay, and so is my film class. But I still don't know what I want to major in."

"Wait and see. Keep looking. You're only a freshman, you know."

"That's what Josh told me the first time I met him," Winnie remembered.

Her mom leaned over the table with a knowing smile. "Josh?"

"He said freshman year should be about figuring out what you want to do."

"Winnie, who's Josh?"

"Oh. This guy in my dorm."

"Sounds like an interesting guy."

"He is. Especially considering he's just a freshman, too." Winnie covered her face, then grinned at her mother. "He's a computer major who lives down the hall."

"Do you like him?"

"I think he's great."

"Then he probably is."

"He's incredible, Mom. He's funny and smart and thoughtful, and even a little flakey—like me."

"I'd like to meet him."

"Maybe you will," Winnie giggled.

Then Winnie's mom put a hand to her mouth, as if she'd just remembered something. She reached down for her big canvas handbag and began sorting through it.

"I almost forgot," she gasped, taking out cosmetics, scribbled envelopes, appointment cards, and Parents' Visit brochures. Finally she found a packet of letters, which she placed on the bar between their platters of sushi. "If you're as interested in this Josh person as I think you are, you may not want to look at these."

"What?"

"These letters. They arrived for you a few days ago. It looks like they've been lost in the mail for some time."

Winnie began to flip through the stack, which included postcards, overseas letters, and a note written on the back of a cardboard menu. Just seeing the handwriting sent a jolt through Winnie. She checked the signature. Once. Twice.

Travis Bennett.

Still, Winnie couldn't believe that the letters were really from him. After all this time, it was overwhelming to think that she had heard from Travis again.

"Are these all from who I think they're from? That boy from Seattle you met in Paris last summer?" her mother asked.

Her pulse on overdrive, Winnie flipped through the letters again. Then she nodded. "I can't believe it. I thought he dumped me. I thought I'd never hear from him again."

"Well, Win, I guess you were wrong."

Winnie was still staring at the correspondence. She skimmed a few postcards and got the general gist of Travis's messages. He'd written to her starting on the day he left Paris. The two early notes were love letters, then his message became confused. The final note accused Winnie of not caring enough to end things honestly. And every one of Travis's letters had been sent to the wrong Paris address.

"Why didn't I get these letters over the summer?" Winnie cried.

"There was a mixup, Win."

"How did they finally get to me after so long?" Winnie had felt that her whole summer abroad had been a disaster, because she had fallen so hard for Travis Bennett and then been dumped. But it now looked like Travis had assumed that he'd been dumped, too.

"I think they eventually got back to the Teen Summer Abroad office, and they finally sent them back to me." Winnie's mother smiled. She leaned over the counter. "What are you going to do about it?"

"I don't know," Winnie breathed, staring at the stack of letters. She picked them up and waved them in front of her. "Aggghh! Travis Bennett. What are you doing back in my crazy life!"

# Six

•••••••••••

auren had never enjoyed a sorority house-decorating session so thoroughly. She made perfect paper flowers. She cut crepe-paper streamers that were all exactly the same length. She smiled and pretended that prettying up the Tri Beta sorority house for Parents' Open House was the most important endeavor in the world.

"I didn't expect you to be so into this," commented Marielle Danner, Lauren's appointed Tri Beta big sister. "Especially after everything else you've been doing lately." Marielle was very thin. She wore chunky charm bracelets and bright red lipstick and had an insistent Southern drawl. "I wondered if you would even show up today."

"Of course I showed up. I wouldn't miss this."

Lauren put the crepe paper back on the antique library table. Even though the Tri Beta president, Courtney Conner, had been impressed with Lauren's involvement in the Bickford Lane demonstration, Lauren knew that Marielle still thought of her as an overweight dud. But for once Marielle's snobbery didn't bother her.

"I'm glad your attitude is improving, Lauren. Because you have missed required events in the past, you know."

"I know, Marielle. I'm so sorry," Lauren lied.

"Saying 'I'm sorry' is easy," Marielle reminded her. "Actions are what count."

Lauren made five more perfect paper flowers. No matter what Marielle said, Lauren knew she could take it because she also knew she wouldn't have to listen to Marielle much longer.

"I'm done with the flowers," Lauren announced. "Shall we go in the kitchen and help with the cupcakes now?"

Marielle gave Lauren a slightly suspicious glare, as if part of her couldn't believe this new Lauren was for real. "Good idea," she finally said.

They walked across the Tri Beta living room, past the floral bouquets and the crackling fire. In the kitchen the cook was making little turnovers, while a group of pledges decorated an elaborate spirit cake decorated in the school colors.

Lauren and Marielle sat at a small table, in front of a silver tray of plain cupcakes and bowls of colored frostings. Marielle reached into the cabinets and took down containers of colored and chocolate sprinkles.

"Please use mainly the school colors," Marielle instructed.

"Of course." Lauren began to frost and sprinkle.

"I must say, Lauren," Marielle informed Lauren as she worked, "your clothes aren't so bad today. You still could use some more color, but at least you don't look like you've been shopping at the Salvation Army thrift shop anymore."

"I'm so glad you think I look better, Marielle." For the decorating session, Lauren had changed back into the plain, good-quality woolens her mother had bought for her. At first, her new bohemian clothes had made her feel like she was in disguise. Now it was the beige cashmere that felt like a costume.

Marielle picked up some sprinkles with a wet fingertip and nibbled them off. "I know I've been critical of you, Lauren. But that's just the way I am. I can't help it. I'm an honest person. I have to let a pledge know when she's in trouble. I'm also the first one to let a girl know when she's improving."

"Thank you so much." Lauren pushed up her sleeves and frosted another cupcake.

"You're welcome."

Lauren suppressed the urge to smile. "I know Parents' Open House tomorrow is important, and I want to make sure that I give the right impression." Lauren felt like she was reading from a script. Her tone was ultra-syrupy. "And then there are all the frat parties tomorrow night after the Civil War football game. I've been thinking about my clothes lately. I want to look good so the Tri Beta sisters will be proud of me."

Marielle tossed back her straight hair. She looked at Lauren with new respect. "You know, we've all been invited to the frat party at the Sigma Theta house tomorrow night. I guess the Sigmas are throwing their party especially for us. Are you coming? If you want, I'll even fix you up with someone."

"That's okay," Lauren came back quickly. "I'll just make an appearance as a Tri Beta and then go back to the dorms. I have a lot of homework." Actually, Lauren and Dash were planning to roam Greek Row, looking for anything that might make a hot exposé for the newspaper. But they had no idea where to look, or if there would even be any hazing taking place. With that purpose in mind, Lauren continued her act for Marielle. "You know, I've heard that at some of the frat parties after the Civil War game, things can get pretty raunchy. Do you think the Sigmas will do anything like that?"

Marielle shrugged.

Lauren pressed on. "I guess no one hazes anymore, do they?"

Finally Marielle broke into a smirk. "I wouldn't say no one. You know how guys are."

*Not all guys,* Lauren wanted to argue. She couldn't imagine Dash bullying some poor pledge just because he wasn't macho or cool. "You mean it's true? Pranks do get carried out after the Civil War game? But I thought hazing was illegal."

"Don't be so naive. Of course it's true." Marielle stuck a finger in the frosting and began to lick. A big grin covered her pretty face. "Lauren, can you keep a secret?"

Lauren nodded.

"I guess I can tell you. Our fearless leader, Courtney, is always telling me I have to include you in more things." Marielle moved closer. "But if you blab this to anyone, you'll be automatically kicked out of our house. You know that, don't you?"

Lauren tried to look worried. "Of course."

"Okay. Well, I don't know about the Sigmas, but a hunky guy I know at another frat house says there is something really vicious and wonderful planned over there tomorrow night." Marielle giggled. "There's this totally pathetic geek of a pledge they want to get rid of. You won't believe what they're going to do."

"What?" Lauren stayed cool, even though she was dying to find out which house Marielle was talking about.

Marielle looked coy.

"Which fraternity?" Lauren prodded.

Marielle stared at Lauren for a moment, then pulled back. For a moment Lauren feared that she'd been found out.

"I can't tell you," Marielle decided. "Not that I don't trust you, but I made a promise, too. I just wish I could see what those guys are going to do."

"Why can't you?"

Marielle huffed. "Courtney will have a cow if we don't all show up at the Sigma house. I mean, we're welcome at any frat house on the row, but you know how Courtney likes to tell us all what to do."

Lauren crossed the Sigma house off her and Dash's list. But that still left fourteen other frat houses on the row.

Marielle looked up at Lauren and stared again. Suspicion came back into her eyes. "Why did you ask about hazing?"

"No reason," Lauren chirped as she spread frosting on another cupcake. She suppressed the urge to squish the cake on Marielle's head, and instead placed it back on the shiny silver tray.

"I'm late, I'm late, for a very important date."

At the day-care center that same afternoon, Faith had been put in charge of storytime again. She'd read *Alice in Wonderland* until the kids had gotten restless. Out of desperation, Faith had organized them into a little play instead.

"Good, Jeremy," Faith encouraged. "You remembered your lines. You keep being the White Rabbit. Just say that same line over and over."

Jeremy nodded, then made his descent down the rabbit hole, which consisted of four preschoolers lined up and arched over the floor. Katie, the red-haired girl enacting Alice, scrambled after Jeremy and followed him down the hole. Amid the splash of colors from the construction-paper cutouts and the decorated bulletin boards, the kids were taking their play very seriously.

"This is too cute for words," grumbled Marlee, the sole audience member, who was sitting in the corner on a chair that was much too small for her. Faith's co-workers, Chip and Shelley, were in the back bandaging a kid's knee, while Faith and Marlee's parents were spending the afternoon at a series of special lectures on financing higher education. They'd convinced Faith to take Marlee along with her to the day-care center.

Faith ignored Marlee's comment. "Okay, Ruby," she instructed a chunky girl who wore thick glasses and a frilly pink dress, "can you be the garden wall? Miles and Nell, can you help her? The rest of you can be flowers and insects."

While the kids scrambled and buzzed about, Faith turned back to her sister. So far she'd been too crazed with her parents, Christopher, and classes to spend much time with Marlee. But Marlee seemed to be growing more sullen by the second. She was slumped in the tiny chair, wearing her rock logo jacket, black jeans, and black boots that needed polishing. Faith was the most sympathetic person in the world, but between Christopher and Brooks, she didn't have much energy left.

"Marlee."

"What?" Marlee demanded, finally looking up and meeting Faith's eyes.

"Cheer up. I know this isn't exactly sophisticated college stuff," Faith said, "but it's part of my freshman year. Believe it or not, during your freshman year, you may have to do things like this, too." Faith was a little embarrassed to have dragged Marlee to the day-care center. She wondered if her sister was watching her, thinking that her big sister was wasting important time. Part of her wished she could tell Marlee what was really going on during her freshman year. "It's not that bad."

"I won't have to do things like this my freshman year," Marlee came back. "Not if I don't go to college and don't *have* a freshman year." Then she played with her long hair and stared out the window.

"What do you mean?" Faith couldn't imagine Marlee not going to college. "I thought you were interested in U of S, and that's why you came along with Mom and Dad."

Marlee shook her head and stared out the window again. "That's Mom and Dad's version."

Faith wasn't sure what was going on. She'd begun to wonder if Marlee had always been this distant and unhappy, or if she'd been having problems at school. When Faith really thought back, she realized that most of her high-school years had revolved around Brooks, drama, Winnie, and KC. Still, she and Marlee had planted a garden together and shared clothes and late-night talks. Marlee had tagged along once in a while with Faith's friends, looking up to Faith, even adoringly sometimes. Faith wanted to sit down and be a big sister to her, but the kids were about to tear the roof off the place.

"Okay," Faith told the children. "Do you want to try the Mad Hatter's tea party?"

They all screamed, *"Yes!"*

"Who wants to be the Dormouse?"

Five kids raised their hands. *"I do."*

Marlee huffed.

"How about if all five of you be the mouse together?" Faith suggested, trying to be upbeat for the kids and Marlee at the same time. "Go in the corner and figure out how one of you can be the whiskers, one of you can be the tail, one the arms, one the nose and one the ears. Got it?"

The five kids rushed to a huddle in the corner, while the others waited to see what they would come up with.

Faith went over to Marlee, but her sister wouldn't look at her, so she glanced out the window. All she needed now was for Christopher to show up. But there was no one in MacLaughlin Park. And Faith knew that if Christopher had any free time, he would probably go to the ODT house or the TV station. Another possibility, she realized, was that he might have gone to the airport to meet Suzanna Pennerman.

But luckily Faith couldn't think about Suzanna for long. She couldn't worry about Christopher or Brooks, her independent study, or even Marlee, because the five kids were running back into the center of the room, ready to show her their group interpretation of the Dormouse.

"Okay," Faith encouraged. "Let's see what you came up with."

The other kids scooted back, leaving a circle for the collective mouse. After a few moments of bickering and confusion, the five kids began. At the same time, they created something Faith could only think of as a Dormouse machine. The whiskers fluttered, while the nose sniffed and hopped about. Meanwhile, the tail slithered along the floor and the ears stood very still, listening. The most mysterious part of the Dormouse was Angelica, the girl who played the Dormouse's arms. She stood stiffly, facing one direction and then the other. Even though Faith wasn't sure what Angelica was doing, the group effect was wonderful. Magical. Even Marlee had lifted her head and almost smiled.

"What are you, Angelica?" Faith asked when the kids cracked up and the general chaos bubbled up again. "I thought one of you was supposed to be the Dormouse's arms."

Angelica stood up proudly. "I wasn't the arms, Miss Crowley. I was the door."

The kids applauded and laughed.

Faith laughed, too, grateful that their play had taken her away from thoughts of Christopher and Marlee for a few minutes at least. She also knew that she'd stretched the kids' concentration long enough and was glad when Chip and Shelley came back a few minutes later and took the kids outside for play time.

"Bravo! That was great," she told the kids as they filed out to the park. "We'll try the Red Queen next week."

The kids cheered and waved, then tumbled out to play on the grass.

Alone with Marlee, Faith smiled and wandered around the center, picking up toys and bits of cookies.

For a while Marlee watched her. She refused to smile back. Faith hadn't remembered her sister's eyes being so sad.

"How sweet," Marlee said. "How perfectly wonderful and sweet."

"What, Marlee?"

"You and those kids. It's enough to make me go into a diabetic coma."

"Marlee, I don't know what you're so negative about all of a sudden."

"You don't know, do you? But it doesn't matter. You'd just tell me to cheer up."

The sisters looked at each other. Finally Faith saw a glimpse of the Marlee she remembered. Behind the belligerence was the good-natured, uncomplicated little sister she used to know. "Marlee, what's wrong? Ever since you got here you've been acting so weird. What's been happening since I left?"

"You wouldn't understand," Marlee snapped. "And it's none of your business."

"Why do you think that?"

Marlee let her hair fall over her face, then backed up to the door of the center. "Because you're so perfect, Faith. You're so good and innocent and sweet. Everything in your life goes just right."

Faith thought about Christopher again and her heart skipped a beat. "That's not true."

"You act as if it is. You act as if you're Miss Perfectly Sweet and Nice and Wonderful. Mom and Dad believe it. Your friends believe it. These kids even think you're wonderful. For all I know, even poor Brooks probably still thinks so, too."

Faith was so stunned, she thought she would fall through the floor. "I doubt that."

Marlee's lower lip trembled with anger, but she continued to talk in a cold and angry voice. "I don't." She turned to walk out. "See you later. I can't talk to you. I'm going back to Mom and Dad's motel."

After Marlee left, Faith stood there shaking, her whole body in a state of shock. She wasn't sure who Marlee was anymore. She still didn't know what to make of Christopher either. Or Brooks.

But the person she was the most bewildered about was herself. Brooks seemed to think she was a sleaze. Her parents thought she was exactly the same Faith she'd been in high school. And Marlee thought she was a perfectly sweet, nice, and wonderful *fake*.

# Seven

Dear Winnie:

Okay. So this is what I figure. It's one of three things. Either you met somebody else. Or you decided that I was a jerk. Or you've been carried off by trolls. I can't believe I can joke about this, but what else am I supposed to do? So this will be my last letter. If you dump this new guy, or change your mind about me, or get released from your captors, you can reach me at my mom's house in Seattle. The number is (206) 555-8972. I'm leaving Europe next week and heading for home. So if you ever do want to find me again, that's the place to call. And if you don't want to find me, well, you can't say I didn't try.

*I haven't forgotten Paris, even though it sure seems like you have.*

*Travis.*

"That's the last letter Travis sent," Winnie sighed, folding up his letter and putting it back in the envelope. "There were five letters in all."

"Mind-boggling," said KC.

Winnie nodded.

Faith tossed back her braid. "And this whole time, Win, you thought that he'd just left Paris last summer and forgotten all about you. What a shocker. How do you know what to expect from anyone anymore?"

The three friends were sitting in the student union, leaning over a plate of steaming nachos. It was early Friday evening and the union was crowded. The walls were covered with spirit signs—Chop Down Evergreen, Show Who Rules the State, Civil War 'til One of Us Drops—that were starting to sag and droop.

Winnie sorted through Travis' letters again. "In some ways I guess Travis was right. I did meet someone else . . . eventually. And after I assumed that Travis had dumped me, I did think he was a jerk."

"What about getting carried off by trolls?" mentioned Faith.

Winnie grinned. "You never know what tomorrow will bring."

"That's for sure," said KC.

Faith nodded.

For a moment the three of them stared down at the table. Then Winnie and Faith dug into the nachos.

Winnie waved a chip. "I can't believe I had to wait to tell you guys all the details about this. When my mother brought out Travis's letters yesterday, we were at that sushi-bar place and I almost gagged on my piece of raw eel—"

"Raw eel?" KC stuck out her tongue.

"Okay, so I'm exaggerating." Winnie grinned. "It was raw tuna. Anyway, I almost gagged on my raw tuna. I was totally shocked. I'd thought I'd gotten over Travis, and it was so bizarre to think about him again. Seeing his letters was like having his ghost appear at the sushi bar."

Faith laughed.

Winnie played with her long earrings and chattered on. "I wanted to tell you guys right away and read every letter to you, to get your interpretations and all, but then it seemed like there were parents everywhere. And even though my mother is the hippest adult in the world, this still isn't the kind of thing you want to talk over in great detail with a parent."

KC nodded.

Barely stopping for breath, Winnie reached for another handful of cheesy chips. "Do you realize that this is the first normal, non-parents' conversation we've been able to have in two days? I've been so revved up to talk to you."

"That's kind of obvious," Faith commented, smiling at KC.

"Yeah, Win," said KC. "Your motor mouth is definitely in tune."

"Very funny." Winnie chucked a piece of chili pepper at KC. "Okay. So what should I do? Should I call Travis in Seattle after all this time? Or should I forget about him and just think about classes and my history paper and Josh, who I've decided is the best freshman guy on this entire campus?"

"Something tells me you're exaggerating again," KC warned.

"I'm not, actually. Not this time." Winnie stopped eating and sat back. For once her puckish face looked serious. She smoothed down her spiky hair. "Since I got these letters from Travis, I've been thinking a lot. I really like him."

"Which him?" Faith asked.

"Yeah. Which one do you really like, Win? Travis or Josh?"

"Josh!" Winnie stuffed her face again. "Travis. Both of them. I don't know." She licked salsa off her fingers, then made a face. "I guess we shouldn't eat so much, since we're all going out to dinner tonight."

"You're the one who's eating for three," KC pointed out. She'd been sitting upright in her dark blazer and skirt. So far, she hadn't touched a thing.

"Yeah, well, I'm also the one who ran five miles today." Winnie flexed her bicep. "As you will recall, you two sloths were busy."

Faith sighed. "There's been a lot going on for all of us, Win."

"I know. Hey, did Christopher jump out from behind a lamp post to visit you again?"

"Not today." Faith tried to smile. "Suzanna is probably here for the weekend."

Winnie touched Faith's hand. "Are you okay talking about this? I don't want to make you cry like I did when we were doing our laundry."

"You didn't make me cry," Faith assured her, even though a hint of tears was in her voice again. She took a deep breath. "I'm okay. But there is something new."

Winnie grinned. "Tell, tell."

"Okay." Faith hesitated. "Christopher wants us to spend a night next week at his friend's cabin."

KC stared. "You mean you and Christopher?

Spending the whole night at some little cabin together?"

Winnie gasped. "Oh my God! Are you going to go?"

Faith shrugged.

*"Faaaith!"* Winnie and KC said worriedly at the same time.

KC shook her head. "Faith, are you sure about this?"

"What about Suzanna?" Winnie couldn't help asking. She looked to KC to see if she'd opened her big mouth too far again, but this time KC seemed even more concerned than she was. "I mean, I know I'm not one to give advice about men, but at least I've learned one or two things, like how much it hurts to get that involved with a guy and then decide you made a mistake. Don't you think he should break up with Suzanna first?"

Faith covered her face with her hands. "I don't know what to think. I told him I'd go. Part of me wants to go, and part of me doesn't."

KC reached across the table and grabbed Faith's hand. "You should tell him he has to break up with her, Faith. Tell him that if he doesn't, you don't want to spend the night with him. If he's asking you to take that step, he should make some kind of commitment, too. You should make it a question of Suzanna or you."

Faith shook her head. "I don't know."

KC sighed and finally munched one nacho. "I know that's easier said than done. Actually, I'm not doing too well in the relationship department these days either."

"Let's talk about something else," Faith begged.

They sat quietly, eating chips, until Winnie changed the subject. "Hey, Faith, what's with Marlee? Isn't she being pretty grumpy? I don't remember her being like that when we were in high school. Do you, KC?"

KC shook her head. "I just remember her thinking Faith was so great all the time, and trying to tag along when we went to the mall or Lassen Lake."

Faith checked KC's watch. "I asked my parents if anything was going on and they said nothing was wrong. I want to be a big sister to Marlee and really talk to her, tell her that she can tell me anything, that things are pretty intense for me right now, too. But she thinks I'm perfect. How do I tell her that I understand because I have problems, too?"

"You just say it," Winnie advised.

Faith huffed, pushed back her chair, and stood up. "We should probably get going. We're all supposed to meet at that restaurant downtown at seven."

KC picked up her briefcase, while Winnie stuffed her letters back in her carpetbag and looked down at her purple unitard. She was still wearing her muddy running shoes and her sweatband. "I guess I should go back to the dorm and change my clothes. Even my mother will raise an eyebrow if I show up at dinner dressed like this. Should we all go back to the dorms?"

"I'm supposed to walk off campus and meet my parents and Marlee at their motel first," said Faith.

"I'll go back to the dorms with you, Win," offered KC.

Winnie grabbed KC's arm. "Good. I may need moral support if I run into Josh with these letters on me." They strolled out of the student union, past the janitor and a few grad students scribbling and drinking coffee. "Josh will probably take one look at me, and I'll just blab the whole thing. Or he'll sense it, like ESP."

"Win," KC reminded her, "you're exaggerating again."

"I know." Winnie laughed. "My mother says I just like to make things into big deals. But this is already such a big deal, I don't know if I need to make it much bigger."

They walked out, past the outdoor tables and the kiosk covered with notices. In her excitement, Winnie hurdled over a bench. It was near dusk and the walkway lights were already on. Avoiding a trio of cyclists, they took a detour across a damp lawn until they reached the library.

KC hesitated before parting from Faith and heading back to the dorms. "You know, I wish I was really excited about something right now," she confessed, watching Winnie bounce on her running shoes.

"Like what?" Winnie teased happily. "Making a killing in the stock market?"

KC brushed back a stray dark curl. "Right now I might even settle for two guys being wild about me. I'd settle for one guy."

"Well, I don't know if Josh is really wild about me. I know I'm wild about him."

"I'd settle for anybody being wild about me." KC hugged her briefcase and shivered. "I've been thinking, too, Win. Everybody seems to hate me right now."

"We don't," Winnie assured her.

"Who hates you, KC?" asked Faith. "No one hates you."

"My dad's mad at me. Steven hates me. Lauren hates me." KC groaned. "If one more person looks at me the wrong way, I think I'm going to have a breakdown. I'd settle for someone just thinking I'm a normal human with feelings instead of a monster with a heart made of ice."

"I think you're normal." Winnie hugged her. "Of course, anyone seems normal compared to me."

"Don't worry," said Faith, putting her arms around KC, too.

"Don't worry," KC repeated. "How can I not worry? What am I supposed to do!"

Winnie looked KC right in the eye. "You want an answer? A real, non-motor mouth answer?"

"Sure."

"Okay. Here goes. Maybe if all those people are mad at you," Winnie suggested, "you should just make up with them."

KC frowned. "I'm not ready to make up with Steven. He thinks we can forget everything that's happened and just be friends, but I don't. And I can't make up with my dad. If I do, he'll jump right in his van and be here in two hours."

"What about Lauren?" Faith said.

KC cringed.

"We all need to start somewhere, KC," Faith insisted, turning away and looking off toward Fraternity Row.

Winnie nodded. "Faith's right, KC. Maybe you should start with Lauren."

Faith knew she needed to start somewhere, too. Fraternity Row was on the way to the Mountain Travel Lodge, where Faith's folks and Marlee were staying. But after leaving Winnie and KC, Faith realized that even if the row had been blocks out of her way, she still would have found herself standing in front of Christopher's fraternity, the ODT house.

The doors to the frat house were propped open and, like the rest of the houses on Greek Row, it was buzzing with activity. The porch lights were on. Two ODT brothers were hanging a Welcome Parents banner across the porch. Past the columns, through the front window, Faith could see guys moving furniture and doing last-minute set-up for what looked like a big open house.

Faith stood on the sidewalk and stared down. KC and Winnie's warnings rang in her head. It was a huge step she was thinking of taking with Christopher. Sure she was infatuated with him, so swept away that she was willing to play by his rules. Maybe that was why she couldn't open up to Marlee. How was she supposed to be the wise big sister, and then admit that she was about to do something even though she sensed that it was dumb, even dangerous? Maybe KC was right. Maybe Brooks was right, too. Maybe even Marlee saw through her, and knew that Faith wasn't as sweet and wonderful and happy as she seemed.

When Faith looked up again, she saw a beefy,

well-built guy backing out of the ODT door and running out onto the front lawn.

"Geisslinger is going out for the pass," the guy yelled. "He slaughters the wimp from Evergreen, pummels him, decimates him, wipes his face in the mud, then gets up and catches the long bomb."

A sack of trash was pitched out of the ODT doorway. The guy on the lawn pretended to swerve and evade imaginary tacklers. He caught the trash bag like a football, pretended to throw it at a passerby, then took it around the side of the house. A moment later he reappeared, empty-handed, and went back inside.

"Mark Geisslinger," Faith remembered, even though she hadn't seen Mark since orientation week. Mark was Christopher's roommate. He was a handsome upperclassman with a bushy dark mustache and eyes that had made her feel like something on display. He'd set up Lauren for a cruel prank during rush and Faith sensed that he was capable of even worse. Faith stepped behind a parked car, and thought of leaving the row and going straight to her parents' motel.

"Come on," she told herself. "Listen to KC. Even Marlee was trying to tell me something. I'm too sweet and wimpy to be true."

Faith walked out from behind the car, approached the ODT house, and peered inside one of the windows. This time she saw Christopher walking into the living room. Mark had gone back inside and the two roommates came together for a powwow. They were joined by a third person, a slender girl wearing a dark suit and high heels.

"Suzanna," Faith gasped. The tightness zinged through her again, and for a moment it was hard to breathe. She'd been wanting to meet Suzanna. She'd had visions of Suzanna as an incredible beauty.

Faith neatened her braid and wondered if she looked like a corny freshman in her denim skirt and lacy top. She told herself that it didn't matter how she looked, and forced herself to walk up to the frat-house door.

"Hello?" Faith called in a nervous voice. The guys who'd been pinning up the banner had left. Christopher, Mark, and the girl were too involved in their conversation to notice her. Mark was describing something and the girl was laughing loudly.

Faith slowly walked in. The living room was crowded with folding chairs and cleaning supplies. The guys who had been cleaning up were back in the kitchen now, singing along with some rock tapes while they worked. Christopher, Mark, and the laughing girl were the only ones there.

The girl noticed Faith first. For one scary, electric moment, she and Faith stared at one another.

"Can we help you?" the girl finally asked in a lazy drawl. She shook a charm bracelet, then pushed back her hair, which fell in a straight line across her face. She wasn't a fabulous beauty, but she was chic and attractive, with a turned-up nose and peachy skin.

That was when Christopher looked up as well. His hair was wet and he was wearing a crisp white shirt with the collar unbuttoned over a pair of U of S sweat pants.

"Hi," Faith whispered.

Christopher looked confused for a moment. Then his mouth fell open and his usual charm faltered. "Oh. Faith."

Part of Faith wanted to run out, to say, *Sorry, my mistake, forget all about this surprise visit. I'll never do it again.* Instead she walked up to the girl and stuck out her hand. "I'm Faith Crowley."

"I'm Marielle Danner." Marielle stared at Faith's hand and took a step back. "Do I know you?"

"You're Marielle? You're not . . ." Faith's heart skipped a beat. She wasn't sure if she was relieved or disappointed to find that it wasn't Suzanna. She remembered that Marielle was Lauren's Tri Beta big sister. Although Faith had never met Marielle, she'd heard from Lauren that Marielle was the nastiest snob on Sorority Row. "You know my roommate."

"Who's that?" Marielle asked.

"Lauren Turnbell-Smythe."

"You room with Lauren?" Marielle rolled her eyes and turned away. "Goody for you."

Mark looked back and forth between Faith and Christopher with knowing eyes. He seemed to get some silent communication from Christopher and said, "Come on, Marielle."

"What?" Marielle demanded.

Mark led Marielle to the front door. "I'll tell you the rest outside."

Marielle looked back, trying to figure out what was going on. Then she seemed to decide that Faith wasn't worth her effort and leaned into Mark. "Come on, Mark," she giggled, taking his arm. "Tell me everything about what you guys are going to do tomorrow night. I just wish I could be here to see it."

"I bet you do."

"Mark!"

Marielle's cackle faded away. Christopher and Faith stood on either side of a stack of folding chairs, staring at each other. Christopher cleared his throat. For the first time, Faith didn't fall into his arms right away. She didn't budge. She tried to figure out why she'd come and what she was going to do next.

"Is something wrong?" Christopher asked.

Faith wasn't sure how to answer. She watched a

drop of moisture roll down Christopher's forehead
and wondered if it was water or nervous sweat.

"No. I don't think so," she mumbled.

"Why are you here, Faith?"

"Isn't this where you live?" she answered.
"Shouldn't I visit you where you live?"

Now it was Christopher who wouldn't answer.
He sat on the arm of an old leather sofa. "Is the
day-care center working out any better?"

Faith wondered if she would leave the frat house
without ever mentioning Suzanna's name. Maybe
Marlee was right. She *was* perfect—a perfect door-
mat. "It's a little better. I had five of the kids act out
the part of the Dormouse together—out of *Alice in
Wonderland*—and it was terrific. I mean, I know
they're only kids, but it was great to watch them."

"Good," Christopher said flatly. He looked
around as if he feared that someone would come in.
"I told you it would get better, didn't I?"

Faith nodded, then their eyes locked and she felt
herself take a step toward him. She wanted to feel
the coolness of his pressed cotton shirt, to smell his
clean skin and wet hair. She sensed that he was
thinking the same thing. Nonetheless, she called up
every ounce of courage.

"Christopher, I've been thinking about next
Wednesday night," Faith said. "I know I said I
wanted to go to Jamie's cabin with you, and I do.

But I can't get . . . well, more involved unless something changes with Suzanna."

Christopher tensed. "What do you mean?"

Faith drew up every ounce of courage. She thought of how much it would mean to her to spend a night with him, and knew that it had to mean something deep and real. "It's either Suzanna or me. I can't forget about her anymore. You have to decide." Her heart raced as she waited for him to respond.

Christopher thought for while. He rubbed his hand over his face.

"Christopher," she pleaded. "Say something."

Finally he said, "Okay. You're right. I've put this off long enough. Suzanna's arriving tomorrow morning. We're supposed to go to the game and she plans to stay the whole weekend, but I'll tell her before. I'll break up with her as soon as she gets here."

He stood up and reached for Faith once more. "Thank you," she cried, and fell into his arms.

# Eight

"verybody must be at the football game," Winnie said out loud.

Forest Hall was quiet. For the first time that Winnie could remember, not a single stereo blared. The walls didn't shake and no one was throwing water balloons in the hall.

Winnie was alone in her room, since even study-fiend Melissa had gone to the Civil War game. Winnie paced. She sang. She tapped a few keys on Melissa's typewriter. When she opened her window, she could hear shouts and cheers rise up from the stadium on the other side of the campus.

"This is my chance," she mumbled, striding back and forth past Melissa's anatomy models and the mess building up again on her own side of the room. "It's now or never." She kicked up a running bra and an empty Good and Plenty box. The box landed in her trash can. "Touchdown!" Winnie cried. Then she collapsed on her squeaky bed. "If I'm going to call, I'd better just . . . call."

Winnie curled up in a ball and moaned. She was in day-glo tights, a crop top, and a fringed suede jacket that she'd borrowed from Faith. Winnie figured she looked like Daniel Boone at an athletic contest. Maybe she needed to be dressed that way, since the call to Travis might be as gut-wrenching as a pioneer journey and as bone-jarring as a fifteen-mile run.

"You're exaggerating again, you maniac," Winnie muttered. "And not only that, you're talking to yourself. You'll probably be the first freshman locked up for laughing at her own jokes."

Winnie jumped up, steadied herself against her desk, and looked at her door. There was a pay phone in the dorm basement, but it was out of order, so she'd have to use the phone at the end of her hall. Unfortunately, Josh lived down that same hall. All Winnie needed was for Josh to walk by just as Travis picked up. If that happened, Winnie imagined she'd probably hyperventilate or go into cardiac arrest. Or even worse, Josh might overhear, figure out she was interested in someone else, cancel their date for Tuesday night, and give up on her. When Winnie thought about that, it hardly seemed worth it to make the call at all.

Nevertheless, Winnie knew that she had to make the call. Travis wasn't just some guy, some summer fling that had faded as soon as they both got back to reality and school. He was much more than that. She'd met him just when her European summer looked like it was going to be a total bust. They'd struck up a conversation about Muzak and rock in a Paris Burger King. Travis was a musician, a year older than Winnie, but even more passionate and impulsive. They'd spent almost a week together in his tiny hotel room, living on coffee, baguettes, cheese, and love.

"That was last summer," Winnie babbled, even as she trudged toward her door and peeked out into the hall. She didn't see a soul. "Why do I have to call him now?"

Winnie knew why. Because she'd loved Travis, even if it had been only for that one week. She'd made love with him, something she'd never done with any other guy. And though her mother had given her birth control when she'd turned sixteen and encouraged her to be adventurous and free, it wasn't until Travis that she'd taken that monumental leap. That was why it had hurt so deeply when she'd thought Travis had taken their romance so lightly and forgotten her as soon as he'd blithely traveled on.

"I can't do this," Winnie groaned, even though she was already halfway down the hall. "I can't!"

But she reached the phone anyway. She took deep breaths. She tried knee bends, stretches, twisting at the waist. Finally she just threw her hands in the air. There were more reasons why she was terrified to think about Travis again. She was beginning to get herself together. Life was starting to turn serious and she was turning serious, too. What if talking to Travis made her so crazy that she started messing up again? Travis's last letter was dated back in August. What if *he* had found someone new or decided that *she* was the jerk? What if he wanted to drop into her life for another five seconds only to disappear again? Winnie had almost gone batty getting over him the first time, and she didn't know how she would handle it if she got her hopes up only to be rejected again.

But Winnie did it anyway. She picked up the phone. It was almost as if her hand had acted without an instruction from her head. She'd memorized Travis's Seattle number and punched it in as she glanced back at Josh's door. Travis and Josh were about as different as two people could be. Josh was warm and absent-minded and funny. Travis was impulsive and hot-headed and romantic. Josh had left a wacko computer message on her door. Travis would have broken the door down and sung a love song, accompanying himself on his bass guitar.

Winnie put her hand over her eyes, but the phone rang and rang and rang. When no one picked up, she began to relax. She told herself that she'd been given a second chance. No one was home. She started to hang up the phone.

"Hello."

Winnie gasped, grabbing at the receiver again. Her pulse had just gone into triple time and her voice wouldn't come out. The phone had been answered by a young-sounding woman. Travis's sister? His new girlfriend?

"Hello?" the woman repeated in a friendly voice.

"Uh, yes. May I please speak to Travis?"

"I'm sorry, he's not here. This is his mother. May I take a message?"

Winnie slipped all the way down the wall until she was sitting on the floor. "Oh," she managed to get out. She cradled the telephone receiver as if it were alive.

"Who shall I say is calling?"

"Um, well, an old friend."

"I see. Would you like to leave your number?"

"Yes," Winnie realized. She checked the hall again. No sign of Josh. "Oh yes."

"Hold on. Let me get a pencil."

Winnie hung on. But before Travis's mother came back on the line, Josh's door swung open. Winnie panicked. She looked for someplace to hide, but there was nothing besides beige walls and closed dorm-room doors. Trying to stow the phone receiver in Faith's jacket, she stared with wild eyes, while Josh's door closed again and his cheerful Japanese roommate, his arms full of books, came out and smiled at her.

"Hi, Winnie."

"Hi, Mikoto," Winnie stammered. "Where's Josh?"

"I guess he went to the game. It looks like you and I are the only ones who missed it."

Winnie nodded.

"See you later." Mikoto smiled and casually strolled out the back door.

"Oh my God," Winnie whispered after Mikoto was gone.

"Excuse me," prompted Travis's mother. "I didn't quite hear you."

Winnie swallowed. Her mouth suddenly felt like straw. "My name is Winnie Gottlieb. I'm a friend of Travis's from last summer in Europe."

"How nice. Where can Travis reach you, dear?"

Without thinking, Winnie rattled off the number of the dorm hall phone. Then she thought about

Travis calling back and Josh answering the call. She tried to figure out how to take her message back.

"I'll give him the number, Winnie," Travis's mother had already chimed. "He's been in and out since he's been back from Europe, playing with his new band. It's hard to pin him down, so I can't tell you exactly when he'll get back to you. You know how Travis is. But whenever I do see him, I'll be sure and tell him you called."

"Okay. Thank you."

"You're welcome. Bye now." Travis's mother hung up and Winnie heard the dial tone again.

*"Help!"* Winnie yelped. She leaned her head against the pay phone as her voice echoed down the empty hall.


"It *was* a great game, Dad," Faith said as she walked off campus with KC and her family after the Civil War football battle. "I couldn't believe we got that touchdown in the last fifty seconds."

"I couldn't believe it either," Dr. Crowley said with enthusiasm. "That was one of the most exciting last quarters I've ever seen."

Mrs. Crowley was all smiles, too. "I never thought we'd make it. Did you, Marlee?"

Marlee ignored her while her father nodded and KC stared at the stoplight. KC realized that the more cheerfully the Crowleys discussed the football game, the more miserable Marlee seemed. They crossed University Avenue with the rest of the post-football crowd and began walking down Frat Row on the way toward the motel.

"It's too bad your folks couldn't come, KC," Mrs. Crowley said.

KC fell as silent as Marlee. During halftime she'd actually started missing her parents. Marlee had made some sarcastic comment about Faith always being right about everything and for a moment it had looked like the perfect Crowley family was going to come apart at the seams. But then all the bad feelings had been zipped back up. And that was when KC had longed for her father, who would have stood up and said, "Whoa, what's going on here? Let's get this out in the open and talk about it."

"Well, my dad's not a big football fan, Mrs. Crowley," KC said. "I think he feels football is too violent."

"I still think he might have liked this game," cheered Faith's dad.

"Maybe you're right." It was weird, but KC sensed that her father *would* have liked the Civil War game. He'd have called the ballplayers "pin-headed hulks," while her mom would have laughed and told KC to loosen up. Her folks would have liked the whole Parents' Visit.

"You know a lot about football, don't you, KC?" said Dr. Crowley.

"Yeah. I guess I'm the competitive type."

They stopped in front of the Phi Gamma Delta fraternity. Some frat guys were throwing a football on the front lawn of the brick Tudor house. There were flowerbeds at either end of the grass that were being used as goal lines. Watching the guys play made KC wonder if she didn't need a new goal herself.

Faith faced her parents. "I guess this is where we say goodbye. Your motel is just down this street. It's been great to see you. KC and I should walk back to the dorms."

Dr. Crowley hugged her. "Well, we had a great time, didn't we, Marlee?"

Marlee shrugged.

"We're proud of you, Faith," Mrs. Crowley added, hugging Faith too. "You've always made us so proud."

"Well, we're going now," Faith said. "Thanks so much for coming. We'll see each other at Thanksgiving."

"I can't wait," Mr. Crowley answered. "You know how we miss you."

"Bye. We love you, Faith."

"Bye. I love you, too."

Faith's parents walked down the street, but

Marlee hung back for a moment. She wrapped her arms around herself and let the breeze blow strands of her hair across her mouth. "Bye, Faith," Marlee finally whispered.

When Marlee turned to join her parents, Faith grabbed her sleeve. "Marlee," she blurted, "if you need to talk to me, call anytime. I know you think I wouldn't understand, but I've been through more than you think, especially since I started college."

KC saw a flash of hope light up in Marlee's eyes.

"I won't judge you or put you down," Faith went on. "I'm not perfect by any means. I've made a lot of mistakes. And I'm here for you, no matter what."

Marlee started to say something, then turned away and joined their folks.

"Wow," KC sighed. "What is going on with her?"

"I don't know. I just know I want to be there for her, if she'd only let me. It's all I can do right now."

KC wondered if that could be her new goal, to be there for people whenever they needed her. No one could accuse her of being heartless if she did something like that. She wondered if being there for her friends could ever make up for Steven and Lauren and her dad.

They stood on the sidewalk for a while, each lost in her own thoughts. Soon the crowd of parents was replaced by well-dressed frat brothers and sorority sisters rushing to well-dressed parties.

"Did you have a good time with your folks?" KC asked.

Faith sighed. "I'm glad they all came, but I feel like I hardly know them anymore—like I hardly know myself."

"Maybe that's what being a college freshman is all about."

"I hope not."

"Yeah, I know what you mean." KC noticed Faith staring at the ODT house. Two guys were hanging a victory banner over the door. Another pair carted in a beer keg, and they could see more ODT brothers inside setting up the stereo.

"Look at that," Faith said, with a catch in her voice. "The guy I'm seeing—if I can even call it that —is somewhere in that house. He's having a big party tonight. Not only am I not invited, I'm sure he doesn't want me within ten miles of the place. But that's okay, I just smile and keep right on seeing him whenever he wants." She covered her face. "And Marlee thinks I'm Miss Sweet and Perfect. My parents are so proud of me. What a laugh."

KC stared at the frat house, too. She remembered the one party she'd attended there. It had been during rush, when KC would have done anything to become a Tri Beta. She'd set up Lauren to be hazed and humiliated. Now that memory made her sick. "Maybe you're lucky not to go to any of those frat parties. Did you ever think of it that way?"

Faith dug her hands in the pockets of her overalls. "Maybe. But I still wish I could go in there tonight."

"Why?"

"Christopher promised he'd break up with Suzanna today. But I wonder if he really did it. He called last night and gave me all the details for going to the cabin, and all I kept thinking was that I wouldn't really know for sure about Suzanna. I hate being suspicious, but I would give anything to be invisible and see if she's his date at that party tonight. That way I'd know if he really told me the truth. I'd know just how sweet—and stupid—I really am." Faith groaned and looked up at the sky.

"You really want to know what's going on at that party tonight?" KC asked.

"I have to know."

If KC could do something for a friend—if she could be there for Faith—that might be the first step to becoming human again. KC didn't want to see Faith get hurt or deceived. Helping Faith find out the truth might not make up for her father, but as Winnie had said, it was a place to start.

"What if I went?" KC volunteered. "I bet I could get in and find out if Christopher and Suzanna are still together. No one ever worries about girls coming to frat parties on their own."

Faith gasped. "You mean you'd go to the party for me and find out if Christopher told me the truth? You'd spy for me?"

KC put a finger to Faith's lips. "Please. Let's call this by a positive name. I want to do something to help you. You need to know about Suzanna before you go to that cabin. And I need to do something special for my best friend right now."

Faith looked at the house once more. "You would really do that for me? As a friend?"

"I can't think of a better reason," KC said.

# Nine

**A**re we winners?"
"Yeah!"
"Did we beat them?"
"Yeah!!!!!"
"Are we the best?"
"Yeahhhhhhh!!!"

After the football game everybody on the dorm green was in a victorious party mood. People were rocking out. Couples tackled each other, giggled, and rolled across the grass. Six dance majors were even improvising a chorus line in front of Faith's dorm, complete with pennants and U of S caps.

Faith smiled through it. After KC left her to get ready for the frat party, Faith turned down offers to play and dance and wrestle. She passed the crowd of singers around the Coleridge lobby piano and made her way up to her room. Even though she kept up her usual cheery front, she wanted to be away from anything that resembled a party. The last thing she wanted to think about was Christopher and what kind of news KC would bring back after spying on the big bash at ODT.

Rattling her keys, Faith trudged past the celebrations until she was standing in front of her door. Unlike Winnie's sterile-looking new dorm or KC's charming old dorm, Coleridge Hall was funky and lived-in. As Faith opened her door she noticed the nicks and the ancient graffiti.

Faith wondered if Lauren would be home. At the beginning of the semester, Lauren had spent a lot of time in the dorm, but since she had gotten involved with the newspaper and the Progressive Students' Coalition, Faith hadn't seen much of her. Faith missed Lauren's sensitivity and her interest in things more important than whose party was going to be the best. Maybe Lauren would have some ideas about the day-care center and Faith's independent-study project.

"Lauren?" Faith asked as she cracked the door open and stuck her head in.

No one answered.

Faith stepped into the room and was greeted by

mismatched dorm furniture, her photos of home, stacks of play scripts, and postcards from family and old friends. Lauren's side of the room was crowded with her TV, computer, microwave, CD player, and a few *New Yorker* cartoons.

"Left with my own thoughts . . ." Faith whispered.

She pushed open her window so she could hear the hoots and giggles out on the green. The longer she sat alone, though, the more her head ached with thoughts she didn't want to be thinking. She had visions of Christopher and Suzanna, their arms around each other, while she sat at the day-care center picking up pieces of soggy graham cracker and reading to the kids.

"Maybe I should go to a dorm party. Or listen to the singers in the lobby. Or work on my independent-study proposal. Something!"

Faith finally decided to call Winnie, and got up to head out into the hall. When she opened her door, she felt the weight of someone pushing it open from the other side.

"Winnie?" Faith asked hopefully.

When there was no answer, Faith assumed that it was Lauren after all. Then she remembered that for some reason Lauren was spending the evening with Dash on Frat Row. Faith thought of Christopher, and even Brooks as she swung the door open. But the one person she hadn't expected was the slim, pale-faced teenager she saw outside her door.

"Marlee!"

"I know you don't want me here," Marlee said defensively.

"What are you doing back?"

Marlee's complexion went from a cloudy pink to a drained white. Her eyes narrowed, but before the tears came she rushed past Faith, dropped her over-night bag, and threw herself down on Lauren's bed.

"Where are Mom and Dad?" Faith asked, leaning out to look down the hall. The only person she saw was Kimberly, the dance major from next door. "I thought you were all going home."

"They went home," mumbled Marlee.

"What?" Faith closed her door and leaned against it. "Without you?"

"You heard me. They drove back to Jacksonville and left me here."

Faith was completely stunned. What kind of parents left their sixteen-year-old daughter stranded a hundred miles from home? Certainly not the perfect Crowley parents, or any kind of parents that Faith could imagine.

"I don't understand," Faith admitted. "How are you supposed to get home?"

"I said I wanted to take the bus. I told them to go without me. I refused to get in the Jeep."

"Why?"

"We had a fight. Finally they gave up. I guess they've had enough of me for a while."

"Don't say that, Marlee." Faith wondered how things could have gotten this bad without her knowing about it. "When did you start fighting with Mom and Dad?"

"After you left for college."

"How come I never knew about it until now?"

Marlee looked right at Faith with big, watery eyes. "You never asked. Every time you call you just go on and on about how great being a freshman is."

Faith swallowed hard. She did feel compelled to keep up her wholesome, happy image, especially when she called home.

"I told Mom and Dad I never wanted to be cooped up with them again. They're so phony. When I try and tell them how I feel, they just tell me how you never have problems like mine." Marlee looked up and glared. Her face was so pale and sad that she reminded Faith of those clown faces in dime-store paintings. "Look, I'm sorry I came here and that I had to bother you. I'm sure you have a hundred parties to go to tonight. But I didn't know where else to go."

"I don't have any parties to go to. I said I would be here for you and I am. Marlee, what did you and Mom and Dad fight about?"

Marlee sniffed. "College. They keep telling me how great you're doing here and how college is the answer to everything. Maybe I don't want to go to college at all. I don't know what I want. I know you're having such a wonderful freshman year, but I'm sick of hearing about it."

A wonderful freshman year. This was all so absurd that Faith almost wanted to laugh! Here she was, waiting to find out if the guy she was crazy about was a liar and a cheat, and her little sister thought she was having such a wonderful freshman year.

Marlee let her hair fall over her face. "I'm sick of hearing how great everything works out for you, and how everything I do turns out wrong."

Suddenly Faith exploded. "What makes you think that everything I do works out? What makes you think that I don't make mistakes, too? What makes you think that I'm so perfect and sweet and pure?"

Marlee stared at her with wide, curious eyes. "What do you mean?"

Faith swallowed. For a moment both of them listened to the gaiety on the green and someone practicing a scratchy violin downstairs. Faith felt that horrible tightness again, as if she were being stretched in two directions. Part of her still wanted to be Marlee's perfect big sister. She wanted to be able to say, *Don't worry, you'll grow up to be just as happy as I am.* That was the part of her that still wanted to be the sweet, loyal Faith that Brooks remembered, the part that even wanted to be the innocent little girl her parents still assumed she was. But how could she put those Faiths together with the Faith that wanted to run to a secluded mountain cabin and throw her arms around Christopher? How could that be the same Faith that ached to see Christopher, even though he was engaged to someone else?

"Well," Marlee prodded, "what are you going to tell me? The bus doesn't go back to Jacksonville until tomorrow morning. I have to stay the night here, so I guess we have plenty of time to talk."

Faith took a deep breath and faced her tearful younger sister. As strongly as she wanted to confess everything, to let Marlee know the deceit of her freshman year, Faith turned away and said, "Nothing. I didn't mean anything. I'm having a great freshman year. I'm just worried about you."

Marlee didn't say another word. Instead she began to weep again.

"Did you see Mary Torville with John Lake?"

"I know. Talk about all over each other. I didn't know Delta sisters even dated ODT brothers."

"What do you think of the ODT guys in general? I mean, we are at their party."

The two party girls laughed.

"Hunks. Definite hunks."

"I agree. Major hunks. Except one. Did you see that one guy with the string tie and the cowboy shirt?"

"And that corny beaded belt! If he weren't wearing that belt, I bet his jeans would fall down."

"What would you do if he fell all over you?"

"Gross. His name is Howard Benmann and he's actually an ODT pledge. Talk about geek city. I still don't know how a house like ODT could let a guy like Howard walk in their door."

*Cackle, cackle, cackle.* The ODT party was a buzz of talk. KC had overheard more in one pass through the foyer than she had in six weeks at her study dorm. Of course her dorm had a twenty-four-hour quiet rule, and everybody at the ODT party seemed to be gossiping and chattering as loudly as they could. KC was trying her best to catch every word.

*Somebody has to say something about Suzanna and Christopher,* KC thought. Or she had to run into one of them eventually. KC had seen Suzanna once, so she assumed she'd recognize her—if Suzanna was at the party. And if Christopher had broken off his engagement and Suzanna wasn't at the ODT house, that would certainly be something for people to gossip about. But so far KC hadn't gotten a clue.

She slipped along the back of a couch, trying to stay inconspicuous. She was nervous about being at the ODT party and kept worrying about being snubbed by someone from the Tri Betas. She knew it was pure paranoia, because there wasn't a Tri Beta sister in sight. Besides, KC wasn't part of the sorority game anymore, so what could they really do to her anyway?

Still, as much as KC wanted to come to life and find her soul again, the party got to her. Under the facade of rowdy male raunch, it was elbow-to-elbow class and back-to-back money; good-looking students from good families pushing this way and that way, while trays of chips and crackers were being passed around. The music was loud, but the dancing was controlled and cool.

KC kept cruising. If she couldn't overhear gossip about Christopher, she could only hope to spot Christopher himself. But she'd already been from room to wood-paneled room, and so far all she'd found was a few guys drinking heavily and some couples making out.

That was until she slipped by the library one last time. The door opened and a guy who looked like a freshman nervously went in. A few minutes later he came out again, his face flushed and his composure broken. KC noticed one more guy waiting outside the library door. He was skinny and wore a beaded belt and was sweating so profusely that big drops ran down the sides of his face.

After almost five minutes, during which the waiting freshman practically drenched his cowboy shirt, the library door opened again and an older guy stuck out his head. KC recognized the older frat brother right away. Mark Geisslinger. Mark had been behind that awful rush prank played on Lauren during orientation week. And he roomed with Christopher.

Mark pulled on his dark mustache and swaggered in the doorway. "Howard Benmann," he called. "Guess you're our last pledge. Come on in for your progress report."

The sweating freshman hiked up his pants and disappeared into the dark library. He forgot to close the door behind him and KC stepped up next to the open doorway to spy.

"There he is," she whispered. "At last."

Finally she'd found Christopher. He was inside the library, on the far side of the long table with other important-looking frat brothers. Poor Howard sat in a chair facing them. He was in the hot seat, being grilled about something. This was another Greek ritual, a way of deciding who was good enough and who was not.

KC couldn't quite hear the questions put to Howard, but she saw his pathetic smiles and hopeful gestures, as if he were trying to be cool no matter what. Then he hurried out, looking defeated, as if he'd just been sentenced to execution but still wanted to beg for a pardon.

Howard left the door open again and KC sneaked in. Quickly, she crouched down behind a big wooden bookcase and some heavy velvet drapes. Mark was telling a joke and the older guys were hanging on his every word. They didn't notice KC at all.

"Okay," Mark said, stifling his laughter and quieting the others. "Let's get serious. That was the last pledge. You will all admit, Howard Benmann is a serious problem. A very serious problem."

KC stopped breathing when Mark fingered his mustache and seemed to notice that the door was open. He strode the length of the room and walked right by KC. KC watched his feet as he pulled the door closed again. Mark rejoined Christopher and the others while KC held her breath, praying that she wouldn't cough or sneeze.

Mark ranted, "I don't care if Benmann is the son of a state assemblyman. I don't care if he's going to be a great engineer someday. All I know is that everyone laughs at him. He makes us look like morons and I want him out of this house. As I said, he's a serious problem. And serious problems need serious solutions."

Christopher rubbed a hand over his face. "Why didn't we take care of this during rush? Why did we ask him to pledge if he's such a loser?"

"We made a stupid mistake," answered Mark. "It happens. But now we have to make up for it, or we'll look even more stupid. We have to do something about Benmann before he's an official member of this house. Okay?"

Christopher looked at the other guys. He shrugged. "Look, I know what you guys are talking about and I don't like it. I don't even want to think about it. Especially not right now. This hasn't exactly been the greatest day for me already."

"Okay, Chris," piped up another brother. "We know you broke off your engagement with Suzanna today. But this is important, too."

KC clapped her hand over her mouth. She'd almost let out an audible gasp. Christopher really *had* broken up with Suzanna! She had to repress the urge to run out right then and there and call Faith. Maybe Winnie was right. Maybe the romance between Christopher and Faith was going to work out after all.

Mark laughed. "You should have given Suzanna the dumpola months ago, Chris." He elbowed Christopher. "You want to be tied down about as much as you want Howard Benmann in this house."

All the guys laughed.

Christopher stood up, readjusting his shoulders in his navy sport coat. "All right. Enough about me. Look, you guys do what you think you have to do about Benmann. Just don't tell me about it until it's all over."

"You got it." Mark smoothed his V-neck sweater and smiled. "We won't tell you about how he begged for mercy. We won't tell you about how he threw up all over himself and whined and cried for his mommy."

Christopher frowned.

Mark laughed and told the other guys, "We're going to wait for Benmann at midnight tonight on B Street near Pine. His car is parked there, a seventy-nine blue Volvo sedan. We're going to be there to take him for a ride."

Christopher put his hands over his ears. "If you're going to do something illegal, just do it and stop talking about it so much." He put his hands to his ears. "Remember, I'm on the Interfrat Council. I can't know anything about any hazing."

"Who said anything about hazing?" Mark sneered. "This is just part of initiation. Every fraternity is entitled to initiation. If Benmann can't take it, then he just won't be initiated."

The guys started laughing again. Meanwhile, KC looked for an escape route. She had her information—more than she'd bargained for. But luckily she didn't have to crawl out on her belly or hide behind the curtains all night. Christopher led Mark and his buddies out another door, clear over on their end of the room. So as soon as the library was empty, KC got up and was able to wander back to the party with ease.

She moved through the living room, avoiding guys who drooled over her, refusing to dance when asked. She didn't allow herself to be herded into the kitchen, where kegs were flowing. Her intention was to go right out and rush back to Faith's dorm where she could spill her good news. But something made her linger. Some scratchy little sense told her that there might be even more information to find out.

For almost half an hour KC sat in a dark corner, where guys couldn't harass her. She listened to a trio of Theta sisters rank their pledges. Actually, the Thetas were neither snobby nor mean. They even talked about how to help a certain pledge fit in. But just when KC was getting really nostalgic about her lost opportunity to join a sorority house, she caught sight of Christopher standing lazily in the darkened hall.

KC shouldered her way through the living room, even though she wasn't sure what she would say to Christopher when she found him. All she knew was that she wanted to do whatever she could for Faith again. Squeezing between lovey couples and guys with overpowering beer breath, she walked up behind Christopher and lifted her hand to tap him on the shoulder.

"Oh."

KC's hand froze in midair as she realized that Christopher was not alone. He was leaning against the stairs, towering over a petite blonde with long, dark lashes and a sexy, perky smile. The girl looked right at KC, smiled, and then lifted her hand to touch Christopher's chest. KC knew at once that the girl was not Suzanna Pennerman.

"Of course I know who you are, Christopher," the petite blonde cooed. "Everyone knows who you are. I've even heard you're an intern down at the TV station. I'm interested in TV. I'd love to talk to you about it."

Christopher put a gentle finger to the girl's lips. "Listen, Willa, I don't want to talk about the TV station right now. I don't want to talk about the fraternity. I've had kind of a crazy day and all I want to do is look at you."

Willa giggled and leaned her head back. "Well, look all you want. You can touch, too."

Christopher was already doing that. His fingers had moved from Willa's mouth to her cheek and her hair. KC fought the urge to scream, especially when Christopher turned his head and looked right at her.

KC thought of running and hiding again, and of belting Christopher right in his charming, paper-white smile. But as Christopher grinned at her she realized that he didn't know who she was. He'd only met her once, and even then his eyes had been glued to Faith—just like his eyes were now glued to Willa.

"Excuse me," KC grunted, trying to choke back her rage and disgust. "I'm just trying to find the back door."

"It's that way," Christopher said, pointing toward the kitchen and not giving KC a second look.

But KC had to look at him again. She turned back once, and the last thing she saw before leaving the classy ODT house was Christopher pulling his new, pretty, perky blonde in close and giving her a long, deep kiss.

# Ten

·················

o far we've seen two frat houses get toilet-papered, three guys throw up, and a girl lose her high heels. Whoopee."

"I know, Dash."

"The biggest story we've got is Phi Epsilon's porch falling down and some guy at the Kappa house getting his necktie caught in his zipper. Not exactly the stuff of scintillating journalism."

"You're telling me."

Lauren and Dash sat on the curb in front of the darkened Zappy's Copy Center. They could hear the low din of Frat Row parties a block away and the trickle of water running down the gutter. All evening they'd gone from party to party, watching and listening, trying to scoop out some evidence of hazing. So far they'd come up with zilch.

"Maybe it's too early. It's only ten-thirty," Lauren said. She stretched out and kicked her boots together. She was dressed as half sorority girl, half radical journalist in a cashmere skirt, baggy sweater, and Dash's jacket. "Maybe nothing is going to happen until later."

Dash yawned. In order not to look conspicuous, he was wearing clean jeans with a white shirt and tie. Still, he'd looked pretty out of place on the row, skulking around with his pencil and notepad. "Yeah. Maybe we should keep this up all night. Like a stakeout. I've heard cops sometimes sit for days just waiting for something to happen." His voice had grown flatter with frustration. "I guess patience is not one of my virtues."

Lauren wasn't feeling very patient either. On the one hand, she wanted to get this story even more than Dash did. After all, she was the one who had a score to settle with the Greek system. She was also sure that having her name attached to an anti-frat exposé would be the straw that would finally get her kicked out of the Tri Betas. "Marielle told me that something was planned. I just don't know who's going to do it or where. I'm sorry."

Dash reached into his pocket and took out a stick of gum. "It's not your fault. Maybe it's not even going to happen." He folded the gum into his mouth. "I guess it's weird, being disappointed because some poor pledge didn't get tied naked to a mattress in the freezing cold and stuck in front of the dorms."

"Yeah." Lauren laughed. "We *are* sort of like ghouls, aren't we, sitting around praying for something horrible to happen."

Dash nudged her and grinned. "That's what I like about being a reporter. You never know quite where you stand. You could be doing something admirable, or something despicable."

"I guess I see your point." Lauren never knew quite where she stood with Dash either. Maybe she'd been hoping for a great story to make a breakthrough in their relationship. Realizing what a lame reason that was for going after a story, she stood up and brushed herself off. "Do you want me to drive you home?" Dash didn't have a car, so they'd come in her brand-new BMW, which was parked half a block away.

Dash shook his head. "No thanks. I'll walk."

Dash walked her to her car, then stalled. Lauren couldn't help wondering if this would be the moment when he would finally kiss her. Instead he gave her a light punch in the arm, said goodnight, and strolled away.

\* \* \*

"Marlee. Marlee, please don't cry anymore. Just talk to me. Please tell me something. At least tell me what happened."

"Why? You never tell me anything. Maybe nothing ever happens to you." Marlee was still on Lauren's bed, her neck drooped over like a swan's. She was quivering from her tears. Sometimes she'd slow down and stop, but as soon as she was calm again, Faith would try to talk to her and Marlee would get bogged down in hysterical gasps and groans.

Winnie was there, too. She'd come over to share the news of her phone call to Travis's mother, and to get rid of some of the wacko nervous energy that phone call had churned up in her. She and Faith had Marlee surrounded. Faith kept handing Marlee tissues while Winnie tried to cheer her up with jokes.

"It's a good thing to have some kind of major screw-up while you're still in high school," Winnie soothed. "Honest. Then you're so much more ready for the really big screw-ups when you're on your own."

"Marlee," Faith insisted, "at least tell us what's been happening at home."

Finally Marlee looked at Winnie and sniffed. She turned away from Faith, as if her words were only for Winnie. "Okay. I'll tell you part of it. I was having trouble in my English class. Not that I hate

English, but the teacher was Faith's old drama teacher and he kept talking about her all the time."

Faith and Winnie looked at one another.

"He would always say, 'your sister did this, your sister did that.'" Marlee sniffed. "I tried to complain about it to Mom and Dad but they didn't want to listen."

"Marlee, I'm sorry."

Marlee ignored Faith.

"What happened after that?" asked Winnie.

Marlee rubbed her eyes until they were ringed with watery makeup. "I stopped going to that class. Instead I'd just hang out with some kids on the baseball field." Marlee looked up again, briefly meeting Faith's eyes. "Then I got caught for cutting. The vice principal called Mom and Dad. Dad had a fit and said never to do anything like that again, and then it was over. He wouldn't talk about it. He didn't want to deal with the fact that I wasn't perfect, too. I was supposed to just go back to being innocent little Marlee, sister of perfect Faith."

Winnie sighed. "And I thought I had problems."

"Marlee, is that all that happened?" Faith pressed.

Marlee stared right through her.

Faith tried to give Marlee a hug, but Marlee moved away as there came the sound of a key turning in Faith's door. A moment later the door swung open and Lauren stepped in. Two seconds after that, KC rushed in from the hall, too, took one look at Lauren, and momentarily froze.

Faith stared at KC and Lauren, who were backing into either side of the doorway, waiting for the other to enter the room first. Lauren was pale and soft and determined, while KC looked dark and beautiful and confused.

"What's going on?" KC asked.

"Marlee!" Lauren came into the room and dumped her notebook and purse on top of her TV. "What are you doing here?"

"It's a long story," Faith said.

Winnie stood up to explain everything. "Okay. What's going on is that Marlee is having a major freak-out and got her parents so royally flipped out that they went home without her, which I guess means she has to sleep on the floor tonight and take the yucko, disgusting bus home tomorrow."

"Oh no," Lauren sympathized.

Winnie barely paused for breath. "And I'm here because I called Mr. Wanderlust, Travis Bennett, who wasn't home . . . surprise, surprise. He was out rehearsing with his band, so I had to talk to his mother. She was nice but she sounded like she sees him maybe once every lunar eclipse or so."

Marlee had finally stopped crying and was using the sleeve of her jacket to dry her eyes.

Winnie waved her hands for one last comment.

Her bracelets jangled. "And Faith is here because she lives here." Winnie fell back on the bed and folded her arms. "That's the story with us. What about you two?"

Still in the doorway, KC looked at Lauren again. "I just got back from Frat Row."

Faith shot to her feet. "KC, what did you find out!"

"Well, um . . . Christopher isn't engaged to Suzanna. Not anymore."

"He isn't?" Faith gulped with relief.

"Who's Christopher?" Marlee asked.

"Just the gorgeous guy that Faith is nuts over," Winnie chattered. "They are a très hot and heavy couple."

"Winnie," Faith objected.

"Anyway," KC clarified, "Christopher and Suzanna are definitely a thing of the past. I heard him tell the other guys that he'd broken up with her today."

Faith let out one little gasp, then hugged Winnie.

KC frowned. "Faith, are you still going to spend the night with Christopher at his friend's cabin?"

"What?" Marlee suddenly stood up and pointed at her sister. Her face was red and her swollen eyes were focused with anger. "Faith, you're seeing a guy who was engaged to someone else until today, and you're planning to spend the night with him? Why didn't you tell me? Am I so young and dumb that you had to hide that from me? Or did you want me to be the only one in this family who ever did anything Mom and Dad didn't like, so you could always be the good girl, the perfect one?"

Faith didn't know what to say. She looked back and forth from Marlee to KC. She was torn again, between shame at being caught by Marlee and fabulous joy at KC's news. "KC, are you sure?"

KC slowly walked into the room. "He definitely isn't engaged to Suzanna, but, well, I heard a lot of things." She stuck her hands in her pockets and paused.

Lauren broke in. "KC, you were on Greek Row tonight?"

"Yes," KC shot back. "What about it?"

"Nothing. I was on Greek Row, too."

"So you were both on Greek Row," Winnie intruded. "So were about a thousand other people. What's the big deal?"

Lauren explained defensively, "I was only there trying to find out if any hazing was going on, for a story for the paper."

"Well, I was only there as a favor to Faith," said KC, sounding just as defensive.

"I wasn't there at all, but I would have gone if anybody had asked me," joked Winnie.

Everyone gave her be-quiet looks.

"Soooorrryyyyy."

"This is serious, Win," said Lauren. She put her notebook and purse down on her desk. "I know you think my life still revolves around pleasing my sorority, but I've actually been trying to expose some injustices in the Greek system." She spoke to Faith and Winnie, although her words were clearly for KC's benefit.

"You have?" KC whispered.

Lauren sat down in her desk chair. "At least I was hoping to. I got a tip about some hazing, but Dash and I went to every party we could get into and we didn't see or find out anything."

For a few minutes no one said a word. Marlee glared at Faith while Faith hid her face. KC stared at Lauren while Winnie hummed.

The semiquiet was broken by Lauren, who sat up very straight and announced, "Marlee, you don't have to take that awful bus home tomorrow. Faith can borrow my car and drive you."

KC's gray eyes softened. "You'd let Faith borrow your car to drive Marlee home?"

"Of course I would."

"Lauren, thanks," said Faith. "Marlee, would you rather I drove you home tomorrow in Lauren's car?"

Marlee shuddered and nodded. "Yes. I guess that would be much better. Thanks."

Suddenly Winnie leaped up and clapped her hands. "Okay. Good deal. Now, enough of this misery and moping around. In case you have all forgotten, this is a party night. Not that we want to get wild and crazy or anything, but we can at least get some fresh air and walk around and watch other people get wild and crazy. Maybe we'll even run into wild-and-crazy-and-incredibly-sane Josh." She put a hand to her heart. "Maybe if I saw him again right now, this whole thing with Travis wouldn't seem so scary. What do you say? If Marlee is only going to be here for one night, she should at least see more than the inside of this room."

Faith shook her head. She glanced at Marlee, but her sister wouldn't look at her. "No thanks. I need to think. I guess I'll stand under the shower for about two hours and try and remember who I am."

Marlee coldly moved past her. "If Faith isn't going, then I will. Anything's better than staying here all night."

"I could use some air myself," Winnie chattered, tugging Marlee and leading the way out. "I could stand to use up some excess energy. Maybe I should do five billion jumping jacks, tap-dance on the roof, sprint through the pioneer graveyard, do somersaults in the laundromat . . ."

Winnie and Marlee went down the hall as Faith grabbed her bathrobe and headed for the shower.

KC stalled in the doorway. "Wait for me in the lobby," she called down to Marlee and Winnie. "I have to tell Lauren something."

"Hurry up," Winnie sang.

KC heard the door to the stairwell open and close. Their footsteps faded away. She watched Lauren and cleared her throat.

Lauren barely glanced at KC. She had turned on her computer, and the screen gave off an eerie amber glow.

"Are you coming with us?" KC asked after Lauren brought up a program and typed in a few lines.

Lauren shook her head and kept typing. "I've had enough unproductive wandering for one night. I have a creative-writing assignment due on Monday."

"I understand."

"Do you?"

KC sighed. "I'm not the horrible person you think I am, Lauren. I do have feelings. Believe me."

"Is that what you wanted to tell me?"

"No." KC shifted. "What I wanted to tell you was . . . well, that I appreciate you loaning Faith your BMW. I know you used to feel like some people took advantage of your car and your money. I'm just glad you didn't let that get in the way of helping Marlee. I think she needs help right now."

"Okay."

After a pause, KC went on. "And I guess I wanted to tell you about something that's going to happen tonight on Frat Row."

Lauren tipped her face up. Her violet eyes looked huge behind her wire-rimmed glasses. "What?"

"There's some hazing planned for an ODT pledge named Howard Benmann. Maybe it's the same prank Marielle told you about."

Lauren pushed away from her desk. "Why should I believe you?" she demanded. "Why are you telling me this?"

KC hesitated. "Maybe you'll just think I'm being a rat again, like when I called the police to warn them about your Bickford Lane demonstration. But I don't mean it that way." She swallowed hard. Apologies did not come easily to her. "I mean this to make up for the way I ratted before. To make up for . . . everything."

"You do mean it, don't you?"

KC nodded.

"Maybe you'll save Howard Benmann from something pretty awful," Lauren said. She began searching the room, finding her phone book and a sweater. "That could make up for something, too."

"Maybe." KC knew that Lauren was remembering how KC could have stopped the hazing prank that had been pulled on her.

"KC, can you tell me everything you found out?"

"It's planned for midnight tonight," KC told her. "Mark Geisslinger and some other guys from ODT are going to wait by Howard Benmann's car, a seventy-something blue Volvo. It's parked on B Street near Pine. I don't know what they're planning to do but it sounded pretty bad."

"How did you find this out?"

"I overheard them telling Christopher Hammond about it."

"Christopher Hammond knows? But he's on the Interfraternity Council!"

KC wondered if she was being a rat for the third time. But even if she hadn't had the nerve to tell Faith the whole truth yet, she had no desire to protect Christopher. "Christopher knows. He definitely knows."

Lauren had gathered her things and stood by the door. "I just hope I can reach Dash again." She checked her watch. "If he's not home, I guess I'll just leave a message for him to meet me down there." After her burst of frantic activity, she stood still and looked at KC again. "Thanks. I know it probably wasn't easy for you to tell me this."

"Thanks for loaning us your car so we can take Marlee back to Jacksonville." KC walked slowly out into the hall.

Lauren started to rush out, then said to KC as

she pulled her door closed, "You're going to go home tomorrow, too?"

Until that moment, KC hadn't really considered going along with Marlee and Faith. "I hadn't planned on it. But maybe I'll go to Jacksonville just for the ride."

"Faith told me your folks couldn't come for Parents' Visit," Lauren said. "I remember how weird you used to feel about them. Maybe it will be good for you to see them again."

"I'm not going to see them!" KC argued. "If I go, I'll just go to give Marlee and Faith moral support."

"Okay, it's your choice. It was just a suggestion."

KC looked confused, but Lauren didn't have time to talk anymore. Instead, she left KC and rushed down to grab the hall phone and call Dash.

# Eleven

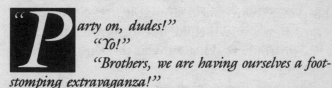

"Party on, dudes!"

"Yo!"

"Brothers, we are having ourselves a foot-stomping extravaganza!"

Christopher Hammond cringed. He knew there were some real animals in his fraternity, but this was too much. It was nearly midnight and the party beasts were acting more and more beastly. They screamed. They sprayed beer fizz. They stomped around, out-machoing one another like competing bulls. Christopher wiped beer foam off his shoulder and thought about how he didn't even want to be at this party. He was there only because it was slightly more appealing than spending the night alone.

"Does that mean party?"

"*Parteeee.*"

"*Parteeeeeee.*"

Despite the fizzing and foot stomping, Christopher could still see the anger in Suzanna's eyes when he'd told her it was over. He could still hear that edge in her classy, controlled voice when she'd told him she'd known he'd never stick it out. He could still hear her telling him how he'd never stuck by anyone, how the only person he'd ever be true to was himself. He could still feel the diamond ring in his pocket, where he'd stowed it after Suzanna had called him a selfish child and thrown it in his face.

"Christopher? What are you thinking about?"

"Hm?"

"Are you thinking about something? I've asked you to dance about five times and you haven't heard me."

Christopher smiled. Even though he kept thinking about Suzanna, he was trying to forget. He was ready to move on. That had been the whole point of picking up Willa, the sophomore he'd found earlier that evening. Willa was cute, with blond hair, a tight, curvy body, and a perky smile. He'd won her over in the first five minutes. And she'd offered a fair amount of diversion since then.

"Do you want to dance, Christopher?" Willa pressed against him.

"If it's okay with you, I'm not exactly in the mood to dance. Maybe later. Do you mind, Willa?"

"Mind? Oh no," Willa gushed. "I don't mind at all. We can just stand here. Or go upstairs. Whatever you want."

Whatever Christopher wanted. So many girls were ready to give him whatever he wanted that he didn't know how he was supposed to stick with one girl—there were so many others that were equally willing. It terrified him to think of sticking with only one girl, forever and ever. How would he ever know that she was really the one? How would he know he wasn't about to turn around, meet somebody new, and realize that he'd made a terrible mistake?

Christopher's parents always talked about how great it was to commit to one person, but they never explained how he was supposed to stay interested after the chase was over. They never explained how to keep from getting terrified when the other person made demands on him and wanted to rope him in.

"This is a great party," Willa cooed.

Christopher put his arm around her and laughed. "Yeah. It is."

Even Faith was beginning to make demands and

rope him in. He sensed that she was truly special, and that his feelings for her were deeper than the feelings he'd once had for Suzanna, but she was beginning to scare him, too. As long as she was happy being in the background of his life, an incredible, exciting diversion, he'd been wild for her. Now he was starting to worry that she'd want the same things Suzanna wanted. She'd want him to be loyal, to be predictable, to love only her.

"Do you want to go for a walk?" Willa asked. "There's a full moon. Or we could go for a ride."

Christopher smiled at Willa. She'd been an easy conquest, and for the moment she was sexy and fun. Maybe that's what he wanted, excitement and passion that could be there when he needed it and would go away when he didn't.

"You want to go for a walk?" Christopher asked, pulling Willa up and slipping his arms around her.

Willa grinned.

But before Christopher could pull her out into the moonlight, he saw Mark come lurching in from the porch.

"Hey, Chris, dude!"

Christopher knew instantly that Mark was drunk. After two years of rooming with Mark, there were few surprises. Mark was one of those guys who took any excuse to go too far. "What, Mark?"

"Wait until you see this," Mark hissed.

"What?"

Mark stumbled, practically knocking Willa down. "Benmann. You gotta see Howard Benmann. Paul and Matt have been pouring beer down him for the last half-hour. I think he's ready for the real stuff." Mark leered at Willa and laughed. "We're gonna walk him down to his car on B Street." He cracked up. "But don't worry. We're not going to let him drive home."

Howard Benmann was someone else Christopher wanted to forget. Secretly, Christopher didn't think much of hazing or picking on guys who were nerdy and weak. But he had to humor the roughhouse traditions.

"Why don't you come, too?" Mark bullied.

How many times did Christopher have to tell Mark that it was against university rules for an officer even to know about hazing? "I can't do that, and you know it."

"Aw, quit drooling over all your women and come with us."

Just then ODT brothers Paul Schultz and Matt Brunengo came in with Howard Benmann draped between them. The sloshed frosh pledge was babbling, his jacket torn and his cowboy shirt unbuttoned halfway down. His legs were like rubber and his mouth hung open. Even though he was barely coherent, Christopher could tell that Howard was still trying to please Mark and the other guys.

When Howard saw Christopher, he pointed at him and slurred, "Is Chrissofer Hammer." Howard crumbled onto his hands and knees and began to bow. "The great Chrissofer Hammammer. King of our great house of Odelta Dekka Cow."

"Get him out of here, Mark," Chris spat out.

Mark shrugged. "Okey-dokey. Outside he goes." Matt and Paul dragged Howard out onto the porch. "If you want to join us later, feel free. We'll be on B Street."

"Right," Chris said. He put an arm around Willa again. "I think you guys can take care of it, Mark."

And then they were gone.

Lauren was behind the bushes.

The big leaves of the hedge she stood beside were prickly and gave off a dusty smell. She tried to part the thorny branches and peer onto B Street, where Howard's blue Volvo sedan was parked in the moonlight near the corner of Pine.

"Oh," she squeaked, pulling her hand back from the spiky hedge. A thorn had pricked her finger. She checked her watch. "Dash, where are you? I can't do this alone!"

When Lauren had called from the dorm, she'd left an urgent message with someone in Dash's house. The guy who'd answered hadn't seemed very clear about whether Dash was home or whether he'd just popped in and gone back out again.

Lauren's heart sped up. She had just heard a collection of male laughs, topped by a slurred voice that sent chills through her. For a split second she popped up and peeped over the hedge.

"Mark Geisslinger," she swore as the gang of guys lurched around the corner. There were four of them. A skinny, young-looking kid—certainly Howard Benmann—being dragged by two older guys, and mustached Mark leading the way with a fifth of whiskey in his fist. Lauren recognized Mark's cohorts from a recent Tri Beta mixer. Matt something and Paul Schultz.

"What are you going to do for the fraternity, Howard?" Mark demanded.

"I'll do anythin'."

"Anythin'," Mark mimicked. *"Anythin'?"*

The guys reached Howard's blue Volvo. Lauren slunk down again.

Matt and Paul sat on the car hood, then pulled floppy Howard up to sit next to them. Howard almost slipped down into the gutter, but the guys pulled him up again as if he were a rag doll.

"Careful, Howie," Mark said sarcastically. He patted Howard's back so hard that Howard nearly went flying again.

Lauren winced. She remembered her own humiliation át the hands of Mark Geisslinger and realized for the first time that she might have gotten off lightly.

"Well, Howard," Mark spoke up, wiping his mouth with the back of his hand, "it's time to really show what you're willing to do for the fraternity."

"I tole you, Mark, I'll do anythin'."

"Will you chug-a-lug some whiskey?"

"Suuuure."

"How much?"

"As muchasyouwan."

Mark gave Howard the bottle and pushed it against his face. The whiskey spilled out of Howard's mouth and down the front of his cowboy shirt. Howard's eyes rolled back and his knees buckled.

"Well, Howard, I'm afraid you've flunked," Mark pronounced.

"Ohmagod," Howard mumbled.

"You're just not turning out to be ODT material."

"I am."

"Prove it."

Howard took the bottle from Paul again, slid down off the car, and tried to drain it. The liquor went down his arm this time, dripping off his pant leg and onto the ground. His whole body had begun to wobble, half collapsing, half performing some kind of weird, exotic dance. Lauren wanted to yell out, *Howard, don't drink any more. Forget the fraternity! Tell these guys where to take their booze and what to do with it.* She'd heard of people getting seriously sick, even dying, from guzzling hard booze like that. But she wasn't sure how much Howard had drunk before this and she didn't know how to stop it by herself.

And if she did stop things, she would have no story. Guys getting disgustingly drunk after the Civil War game was stupid and unappealing, but nothing noteworthy. She remembered Dash's comment about a journalist being admirable and despicable at the same time. All she could do was stand there silently in the bushes, hidden away, and wait for this thing to get even worse.

"All right," Mark said. "Stand him up."

The frat guys shook and clutched Howard until he was almost balanced on his feet.

"Oh," Howard moaned, "I'm sick. Leave me alone. I'm so sick."

Mark shook his head. "Pants him."

Paul lifted skinny Howard and threw him over his shoulder like a sack of grain, while Matt gave Howard's jeans a tug. Howard kicked and grabbed, but he was so skinny that his pants slid right off.

"Get his keys out of the pocket," Mark ordered.

162     •     *Linda A. Cooney*

Matt got Howard's car keys out of the pocket of his jeans, then threw the pants in the hedge, only a few feet from Lauren. He flipped the keys to Mark, who walked around to the back of the car. Meanwhile, Howard was beginning to moan and collapse against the side of the car.

Lauren watched in horror as Matt and Paul stripped off Howard's cowboy shirt. Howard barely stood, swaying and shivering, his body as frail as a twelve-year-old's, while Mark opened the trunk.

"You're lucky, Howie," Mark taunted. "You get to keep your underwear on—for a little while longer." He took textbooks and an armful of tools out of the trunk and pitched the stuff in the gutter.

"He won't need that junk tonight," Mark laughed as the tools clanked and the books fluttered in the wind. "Okay. Let's go."

The other two frat brothers picked Howard up by his bare arms and legs and dangled him over the gaping trunk.

*"No!"* Howard screamed, suddenly aware of what was happening. "I'm sick. *Help! Nooooo!"*

"Afraid of the dark, Howie?" Mark laughed as Howard's delicate body was thrown into the trunk. The three guys stood over Howard, pinning him in as Howard cried and moaned.

"Howard, I thought you were the person who

was willing to do anything for the ODTs," taunted Mark.

"I—I—" Howard shrieked in an eerie, terrified voice.

"Well, you couldn't chug that whiskey."

"I—"

"Howard, we're going to give you one more try. We're going to let you take a ride down the row in your own trunk. Then you're going to get out, stark naked, and walk up to the front door of every sorority house. You are going to introduce yourself and say 'I love you' to every beautiful girl who answers the door. If you can do that—without throwing up or acting like a wuss—you are one cool dude and all is forgiven."

*"Wait!"*

"Bye-bye, Howie."

"Have a nice time in there. We'll see you soon."

"Practice your introductions."

"Don't get lonely."

"Let us know if you want another drink."

Mark directed the other boys to close the trunk. Lauren craned her neck, but she heard only a thud and drunken pleas as Howard disappeared into the darkness. Lauren was really learning what Dash had meant about being despicable. Was she just going to hide behind a hedge while a drunk freshman was dumped in a car trunk and made to humiliate himself in front of every sorority on the row? What if Howard passed out before he even got to the girls' houses? What if he got sick in there? What if there wasn't enough air for him to breathe? Story or no story, how could she sit back and let this happen?

There was a big laugh and when Lauren stood up, she saw Mark and his buddies slapping palms over the hood of the car. Mark dangled Howard's keys and headed for the driver's seat.

Lauren didn't know what to do, but she knew she had to do something. As she watched Mark open the door and heard Howard's muffled cries, she found herself pushing through the thorny hedge. Her skin stung and her clothes ripped, but she didn't care. If anything, the pain only added to her fury. Suddenly she was on the sidewalk, but she didn't know what to do. The guys were getting into the car. She couldn't run the car down, or kick the trunk open. Even if Dash arrived they wouldn't be able to help Howard now.

"Let's go," Mark sang.

Paul suddenly popped out to run around and thump the trunk one more time—and that's when Lauren did it. She didn't know why, she didn't know if it would do any good, but she stood on the sidewalk and began to scream as if she were being torn apart by wolves.

*"Ahhhhhhhhhhhhhhhhhhhhh!        Aghhhhhhhhh-hhh!!!!!!!!!!!"*

"Jeez," gasped Mark, jumping out of the driver's seat.

"What is that?" whined Paul, putting his hands over his ears.

Matt crept out of the car, too, looking just as wimpy and frightened as the rest of them. "Get that girl to stop screaming. What's going on?"

Lauren kept right on yelling her guts out. *"Ahhh-hhhhhhhhh!"*

"Let's get out of here," Mark said, sounding panicked. "Somebody's going to come along and think we did something to her."

"What about Benmann?"

"Just leave him. Let's go!"

Lauren kept wailing until the guys had run all the way around the corner of B and Pine. That was when she saw someone else running toward her, coming from the opposite direction. Dash! Dash had found her after all. He was racing and staring at her, holding his hands out. His face was full of terror.

*"Lauren!"* he yelled, almost as desperately as she'd screamed a moment before.

Lauren stopped yelling and ran to meet him. But then her eyes caught the glimmer of something on the ground. She collapsed on the pavement, stretching her hands out, before she reached Dash.

Dash stumbled and grabbed her. "Are you all right? What did they do to you?" He tried to pull her to him. "Your clothes are torn. Oh my God, Lauren. Why didn't I get here sooner?"

Lauren wrestled Dash to reach further on the pavement and scooped up Howard's car keys, which Mark had dropped and which glittered in the street like gems. "I found them!" she cried.

"What?" He clutched her again and held her against his chest. He was heaving for breath.

"The keys. I found the keys."

"What keys? What happened to you?"

"A guy is in that car trunk. We have to get him out." Lauren tried to get up, but Dash pulled her back down.

"Are you all right?"

She glanced down at herself and realized that she looked like she'd just been in a train wreck. "Yes. I'm fine. Let's go!"

But Dash wouldn't let her up. He grabbed her even harder and blurted, "I got so scared when I saw you screaming like that. How could I let something happen to you? Why didn't I just stay down here all night by myself?"

"I'm okay, Dash. I handled it," Lauren explained.

"I even got our story. We did it. But we have to help that guy—"

And then Dash kissed her, just as fiercely as he did everything else. They came together in the middle of the dark side street, kneeling on the pavement, pressed together as if they were the last two people left on earth. After the kiss, they threw their arms around each other's neck and caught their breath.

As soon as Lauren remembered where she was, she pulled Dash up. He seemed almost as dazed as she was. Within seconds they were running back to rescue Howard Benmann, Lauren holding tightly to Dash's hand.

She didn't know if Dash had kissed her only because he thought she was in trouble, because she'd helped him get a story, or . . . maybe . . . because that was just the way he felt.

She couldn't think about it for long, because she was already pushing Howard's key into the trunk lock. The trunk popped open and soon she and Dash were gently pulling out a weeping, sick, shivering, nearly naked Howard Benmann.

# Twelve

"Jacksonville, I don't remember you looking this good," KC sighed.

It was a little before noon on Sunday, and Faith, KC, and Marlee had almost come to the end of the hundred-and-two-mile drive back to their hometown. Winnie had stayed at school to work on her history paper while KC drove Lauren's BMW past ranches and over mountains. For the first hour, it had been raining hard. Faith and Marlee had slept most of the way, so barely a word had been spoken until they'd pulled off the highway and onto Main Street. Most of the shops were closed, but there was a wet, clean sheen to the pavement.

"How can you say this town looks good?" grumbled Marlee. She sat up and stretched. Her clothes had been slept in and her hair was stringy.

"I guess I've missed this place," KC explained. She felt like crying. Something warm and deep had been tapped inside her. "Hello again, pioneer statue. Hello, Jacksonville Drive-In. Hello, Curl-Up Motel."

"KC, you're really glad to see the Curl-Up Motel?" Marlee groaned. "You're weird."

KC hadn't even wanted to go on this journey, so she had been more surprised than anyone to feel delight at seeing her hometown again. The familiar fire station, the park, the Jacksonville city utility building, and the Big Five hardware store all felt like safe, old friends. As ambitious as KC was, she was beginning to realize that she couldn't cut out the homey, noncompetitive part of her life—at least not without cutting out a big chunk of her heart as well.

"Everything looks amazingly the same to me," said Faith. She peered out the window and rubbed the sleep from her eyes.

"Of course it looks the same," said Marlee. "You don't want to see how things have changed."

"I guess it could look smaller," KC tried to joke. "Like the old elementary-school drinking fountains."

None of them laughed.

"KC," Faith mumbled, "none of this is very funny."

Marlee looked straight at her. "It's sure not funny to me."

KC turned by the Jacksonville Library, heading up a steep hill past big Victorian houses and stocky bungalows with well-kept yards. They slowed down to avoid a kid on a bike. A woman waved as she recognized Faith.

"Sorry." When KC reached the Crowleys' street, she slowed down. "Marlee, do you want to go right home? Or would you rather have me drive around a little?"

Marlee pitched forward in the back seat. As Lauren's BMW crept up the hill, the Crowleys' rambling farmhouse came into view. There was a sign announcing Faith's dad's veterinary office. His Jeep was in the driveway, two cats were asleep on the porch, and a dog and a horse roamed the pasture next door.

"KC, maybe you could just park for a few minutes," Marlee said, her voice starting to tremble. "I guess I'm not quite ready."

"Sure." KC pulled over, a few houses away from the Crowley residence.

"Thanks."

KC turned off the engine, but left the radio on

low. It was tuned to a local station and the DJ was giving a pitch for a nearby auto-parts store.

Faith finally turned around and said, "Marlee, I'm sorry I didn't tell you right away about what I've been going through. I wanted to. But I wanted to be a big sister to you, too."

"Sure." Marlee rolled her eyes. "Anyway, you found out that this Christopher guy broke up with his fiancée, so maybe your life is all hunky-dory after all."

KC started to say something, then stopped herself.

"My life isn't hunky-dory," Faith argued. "Even if things do work out with Christopher, there's a lot more to it. There's my work at college, the theater-arts department, and this independent-study project that I haven't done a thing about. It's not like high school any more. I'm not the person I was in high school."

"Then who are you?" Marlee whispered.

"I don't know sometimes," Faith stressed. "Maybe that's what freshman year is about—not knowing who you are anymore and trying to find out. Maybe that's even why Mom and Dad want you to go to college and not cut classes, Marlee. Maybe they want you to make dumb mistakes, like me, and find out who you are, too."

Marlee shook her head.

"College is a time when you can figure out what's important," Faith argued. "Especially freshman year. Don't you think so, KC?"

KC nodded. "I'm beginning to think that freshman year is a time for learning a lot of things about yourself."

Faith went on making a desperate speech, "Marlee, college is a time to get interested in things —to be committed and explore what you're good at."

"Just like you're so committed to what you're good at, Faith," Marlee spat back.

"What do you mean?"

"I mean, look how committed you are to theater. You're so committed that you just stay in the daycare center and pretend it's fine, even though you obviously don't want to be there. Come to think of it, you're not even committed to those kids, even though they like you so much! I don't think you've really looked at yourself at all."

Faith didn't have a comeback. For a while she sat in the front seat, hugging her knees to her chest and staring out the window.

Finally Marlee said, "Forget it. It's useless to argue about it. I screwed up and it's done with."

"Cutting class is not that huge a deal," KC pointed out. "Almost everyone cuts class one or two times during high school. It's not what I'd call a capital offense."

"KC's right." Faith knelt on the seat to face Marlee again. "Once during senior year, KC, Winnie, and I cut and went up to Lassen Lake to talk about our college dorms."

"You're not hearing me!" Marlee suddenly shouted, slapping the leather upholstery. "You're just like Mom and Dad! I didn't just cut class. It was a lot more than that."

"What do you mean?"

"I mean that when I cut class I hung out with some real loser types. We hid behind the gym and did drugs. But I guess we didn't hide very well because the vice principal saw us and called Mom and Dad."

"You did drugs?" Faith gasped.

Marlee nodded. "I bet you never imagined that would happen in your perfect little family."

"Why didn't you tell me this before?"

"You never would have heard me," Marlee scoffed. "You were too busy pretending that everything was just fine. And when you pretend that things are nice and perfect when they're wrong and painful, things just get worse!"

They sat quietly again while a light rain sprinkled down. A steady *tap, tap, tap* interrupted the radio station as the water hit the windshield of Lauren's car.

Marlee reached for the door handle.

"Are you going to talk to Mom and Dad about what happened this weekend?" Faith asked, stretching out her hand to stop Marlee from leaving. "Or are you just going to assume they won't listen, and let it go?"

"Are you going to tell them that you were seeing a guy who until yesterday was engaged to someone else?" Marlee fired back.

Faith looked stunned. She tried to respond but the words wouldn't come out.

Marlee shook her head, then opened the door and got out. Refusing to look back at her sister, she pulled up her collar and began to run.

"She's right," KC said. "Are you going to tell your parents that freshman year isn't so perfect after all?"

Faith closed her eyes, as if she were fighting one last battle in her head. "I want them to know that I've changed, but . . . Well, Christopher's not engaged to someone else. At least not anymore. So I don't really have major news to tell my folks."

KC leaned over the steering wheel. She knew that she had to tell Faith everything, even though she also knew that it was going to hurt. "Marlee is right, Faith. It isn't always pretty, but we have to face the things that are hard."

"What I've been doing wasn't that bad," Faith ranted. "I never did drugs. I just fell for a guy who was involved with someone else—and now he's free. What if I do stay all night in a cabin with him now? That's not so terrible, not when we love and are committed to each other. Now everything is okay with me and Christopher. Finally, it really is just fine!"

KC couldn't hold the truth back any longer. "No, it isn't."

Faith looked at her with confused eyes.

KC took a deep breath. "Faith, Christopher isn't committed to you. I didn't tell you everything I saw at his frat party."

"What do you mean?"

"Well, Christopher knew that poor Howard Benmann was going to get hazed and he didn't do anything to stop it." KC took a deep breath. "And as I was leaving, I saw Christopher with another girl."

Faith clutched the dashboard and went pale.

"Not Suzanna," KC went on. "Someone else. Christopher was with someone new."

"What?"

"You heard me, Faith."

"Maybe it didn't mean anything," Faith rambled,

as if she were trying to convince herself. "You don't really know what was going on."

KC grabbed Faith's shoulders and made Faith look at her. "Faith, he was kissing her!"

Faith closed her eyes and for a long time sat slumped over, her hands over her face as if she hadn't heard KC, as if she would never hear or see or feel anything for the rest of her life. Silent tears ran down her face and then she began to sob with deep, throaty moans. Her shoulders shook and her back heaved. KC leaned over and hugged Faith as hard as she could.

"It's okay, Faith."

"No," Faith sobbed. "It's not okay."

"It will be okay. You'll get over this and you'll be okay."

"No! I'm a fake," Faith wept. "I'm a sleaze and a fake and a total freshman fool."

"No," KC soothed, hugging her more and more tightly. "No. You just make mistakes, like the rest of us. Maybe Marlee's right. Maybe you need to face more things and admit when they're going wrong, before they get a whole lot worse."

Faith continued to weep in KC's arms while cars drove by and the rain fell softly. Finally she lifted her face. Wet streams of hair were plastered to her temples. Her eyes were swollen and her skin was pale.

Faith rubbed the moisture off the window and looked through the rain toward her parents' house. "Whatever's going on with my folks and Marlee, I guess I should be in on it, too."

"Probably," KC counseled.

Faith hesitated.

"Go ahead," KC said.

"I guess we did tell Marlee the truth about one thing," Faith admitted.

KC shifted back behind the wheel of the BMW. "What's that?"

"That college is about finding out about lots of things. And not everything you learn is going to be nice."

KC nodded. "I'm beginning to think that going to college is also about remembering the people you care for back home."

Faith tried to smile. She reached for the car door, then turned back and touched KC's shoulder. "KC?"

"What?"

"Thanks for telling me the truth. You're a real friend."

KC smiled. "I am?"

The girls hugged each other, and then Faith got out of the car and began walking through the rain.

* * *

Fifteen minutes later KC was walking up to the front door of the Windchime Natural Foods Restaurant. As soon as she stepped into the foyer outside the small, homey dining room and shook the rain off her umbrella, she was reminded of every shift she'd ever waitressed. She thought of all those summers she'd worked prep, making up vegetable broth, whole-wheat rolls, and curried lentil soup.

Sunday brunch was almost over. Only two customers were left, a middle-aged couple leaning on their elbows over empty plates. The rest of the dining floor showed evidence of a busy Sunday morning. Tables hadn't been reset. Menus had been left here and there. KC even noticed a good stack of meal checks next to the calculator and cash drawer.

Her father, who served as host, headwaiter, health advisor, and gourmet expert all rolled into one, bustled out of the kitchen and over to the occupied table. Pouring two mugs of steaming tea, he told the couple that the drinks were on the house, which made the couple clap their hands with delight. Then the three of them bantered like old friends, although KC figured that her father and the diners had never met one another before that day.

As soon as KC's dad hurried back to the kitchen, the man at the table remembered something. He waved his hand, but was too late to get Mr. Angeletti's attention.

KC had told herself that she would never wait on a Windchime table again. And yet, when her father didn't reappear right away, a strong family instinct took over. KC approached the table.

The man looked puzzled for just a moment, as he looked up at KC.

"Can I get something for you?" she asked.

"I decided I wanted a piece of that honey-yogurt pie after all."

"I'll bring it."

The man stopped her. "Are you part of the Angeletti family, too?"

KC looked down at her blouse, scarf, and skirt. "Yes. I'm one of the daughters."

"What's your name?"

KC smiled. "Kahia Cayanne."

The couple smiled back at her. KC bypassed the kitchen, found a yogurt pie in the refrigerator in the back room, and brought a slice out to the customer. After that, she made her way to the kitchen.

Instantly she was hit with a blast of heat and the smell of garlic, tomatoes, and melted cheese. The contrast with the rain outside made the smell even warmer and more delicious. Her father's back was to her. He was alone, whistling and cleaning up.

"How many times have I told you not to run the restaurant all by yourself?" KC ventured.

Her father jumped and spun around. For a moment he looked at her with angry, defensive eyes. Then he leaned back on the counter and nodded. "Your mother just left. She was tired. I like to treat my employees right."

"I'll tell Mom you said that."

"Don't. She'll fire me." He smiled.

KC smiled, too.

"Your customer out there wanted something else," KC said. "I brought him a piece of yogurt pie."

"Is that why you're paying me this surprise visit, Kahia? Because you thought I needed an extra hand?"

"No." KC thought for a moment. "Faith had to drive down here and I came along because I wanted to see you. Um, I wanted to apologize."

"I see." Her father's eyes never left hers. "Have you decided I don't embarrass you so much after all? Or do you feel so guilty about the way I embarrass you that you felt you had to come and apologize?"

KC huffed and turned away. "There's no beating around the bush with you, is there, Dad?"

He shook his head. "No need to hide your face, hon. You never could hide your feelings from me."

"Actually, that's good," she said, facing him again. "That's really good. Anyway, I am sorry. I guess I get kind of caught up in the things that do embarrass me about you and Mom sometimes, and I forget about all the things that are so good." Unexpectedly, she began to cry.

Her dad rushed over and put his arms around her. "No relationship is all good or all bad, hon. All you can hope for is to deal with the bad parts, enjoy the good parts, and stick by one another, no matter what. That's what being a family means." He pulled back to look at her. "We have to be open with one another."

When the embrace ended, KC gave her dad a mock punch in the stomach and smiled. "I guess that means you won't be offended if I'm open with you and give you a little advice, too. A little business advice."

Her dad smiled. "I'm listening."

"Right." KC grabbed a stray order pad and began to write. "First, you have to answer the phone by the second ring—or get an answering machine. Daddy, you can't afford to turn people off before they get here and see what a great place this is."

"You think so?"

"Second, you really should wear a tie and get a haircut. I mean, your look went out with mood rings and bell-bottom pants."

Her father self-consciously brushed back his hair. "I like my hair."

"Third, I know it's your style to be buddy-buddy with the customers, but you can't give things away all the time. You'll go broke that way."

"Okay, Kahia." They both began to laugh. "Okay!"

# Thirteen

........................................

love you, Dennison."

"Amanda, when you took that baby, you ended any possibility of a loving relationship between us."

"Please forgive me, Dennison. You have to understand what I was going through."

"You understand *me*, Amanda. I'm saying this for the last time. If you really loved me, you never would have kidnapped my baby. You never would have hurt me that way. How can I ever trust you again?"

"Can you believe this?" KC asked Faith, Winnie, and Lauren. "I haven't watched this soap opera for weeks, and they're still raving about Amanda and the baby she kidnapped!"

It was Tuesday afternoon, and the four girls were together in Faith and Lauren's room. For the first time in ages, they'd turned on Winnie's favorite soap opera, *The Best and the Beloved*. Winnie was on the floor doing stomach crunches while Faith chewed on a pencil and hunched over a notepad on her desk. KC and Lauren were seated on opposite ends of Lauren's bed, glancing at each other every once in a while, then staring back at Lauren's TV. The scene between Amanda and Dennison faded away, and the corny organ music was replaced by a jingle for breakfast cereal.

KC cleared her throat. "I thought after not watching the soap for so long, I wouldn't be able to follow the story."

"I guess some things never change," Winnie cracked. She put her arms behind her head and began straining her way through another set of crunches.

"That's not true," Lauren whispered with a dreamy expression. She pushed her wire-rimmed glasses against her nose and gazed out over the green. The sun was out and the grass looked particularly bright and lush. "I'm just beginning to realize that things can change all the time."

KC looked at Lauren. For a moment their eyes

met. They each offered half-smiles to the other, then looked away again.

"Maybe we had the right idea at the beginning of the semester," KC offered. "Remember how we were going to meet whenever we could and watch this soap, just so we could check in with one another? Maybe we should think about doing that again." She paused as the cereal commercial faded back into the soap opera. "What do you think?"

"Personally, I've always said that *The Best and the Beloved* was high culture," Winnie joked. She fell back, stretched out her arms, and looked at KC upside down. "I think even my mother would agree that this is an essential part of the freshman experience."

"So we'll start meeting again?" KC asked to make sure.

"But of course," Winnie grinned. She flopped over and looked up at Lauren. "If it's okay with you, Lauren. After all, it *is* your TV."

Lauren took a deep breath. "I'm kind of busy with the newspaper and classes and everything. Dash and I have to write up that hazing article. But I also have a feeling I won't always be so tied up with the Tri Betas. So maybe I could still have time to watch a few episodes a week." KC and Lauren's eyes met again, exchanging a little more warmth and forgiveness.

"Faith?" Winnie checked.

Faith didn't look up from her notebook, but raised a finger to signify that she would show up, too. She went right back to rubbing her forehead and scribbling.

The other three girls watched the soap opera. After a while Freya, the vocal-music major next door, turned a practice tape on full volume and began to sing along. KC turned up the volume and she, Winnie, and Lauren scooted closer to the TV.

"Lauren, how's that ODT pledge, Howard Benmann?" KC asked. "Is he okay?"

"Thanks to you he is. Dash and I took him to the health center as soon as we pulled him out of his car trunk Saturday night. Dash talked to him yesterday and he still wasn't feeling great, but luckily there wasn't any permanent damage."

"I still think that is the grossest thing I've ever heard of," Winnie commented. "Can you imagine being drunk and naked in a car trunk? Talk about surreal."

"Dash and I did some background research and we found that people have died from hazing like that," said Lauren.

KC held her stomach. "It's sickening."

"Is Howard going to be Mr. Brave and let you use his name in your article?" Winnie asked.

Lauren shook her head. "In the article we'll just

call him a freshman pledge. I don't want to humiliate him any more by using his name. But Howard did promise to come forward if anybody tries to deny the story." Lauren glanced at KC again. "I haven't decided whether or not to include the part about Christopher—how he knew what was going to happen and did nothing to stop it. What do you all think?"

They all turned toward Faith for a moment, but she just tensed her shoulders and kept on scribbling.

Winnie switched to leg lifts. "After what KC told me, I personally think he's a royal scumbag."

Faith suddenly bolted out of her chair and put her hands over her face.

"I'm sorry," Winnie cried, popping up also, and draping her arms around Faith. "It's just that I used to be an expert in the scumbag department and I know now it's better to get out and move on—that is, if the scumbag doesn't move on first."

"Faith, I'm sorry, too," Lauren offered. "If you don't want me to include the part about Christopher, I won't. The most important part of the article is that hazing is still going on."

"Do whatever you want," Faith mumbled. "I don't want to think about it. I don't want to think about anything. I told my parents what had been going on when I was there on Sunday and their eyes just glazed over."

"Really?" KC asked.

Faith nodded. "I think it made Marlee feel better, but now I know what she means. My parents didn't listen. Come to think of it, that's how they were when they were here. They even acted as if Brooks and I were still together."

Winnie nodded.

"Anyway, I don't want to deal with Christopher right now—or Jamie's cabin, or Brooks or Marlee or Howard what's-his-name. I'm trying to work up a proposal for my theater-arts independent study. I have until the end of this week, and I can deal with only one thing at a time. I've decided that that's the most important thing right now."

"More important than throwing a pie in Christopher's face?" Winnie blurted. "Sorry. It's just that I wanted to do that to about a dozen different guys I used to know. That and . . . other things."

KC got up and went over to see what Faith had been writing. "Have you thought of anything new for your proposal?" she asked softly.

Faith went back to her desk, tore the top page off her notepad, and threw it in the trash. "I talked to a few girls in the theater-arts department yesterday— some of the freshmen in this dorm who were in the chorus for *Stop the World*. Now that the show is over, they're kind of bored and would like something else to work on. With everything that's been going on, though, it's been a little hard to figure this out. Maybe I should just give up."

"Never say give up," Winnie advised. "Well, say it, but don't do it. If I'd given up every time I'd wanted to, I'd still be in detention after Ms. Merman's eighth-grade geography class."

"I'll figure it out," Faith assured Winnie. "I just need to concentrate on it. I don't want to talk about it anymore."

"Okay." Suddenly Winnie got on her hands and knees-again and crawled right up to the TV. "Oh no!" she squealed, pointing at the screen. "Who is that woman with the sunglasses? It's a new character! *The Best and the Beloved* actually has a new plot and I don't know what's going on." She pretended to faint and fell back. "I knew I'd pay for not watching every day. I knew it!"

"Win," KC warned, "you're even more hyped up than usual."

"I know." Winnie yelped. "I have a good excuse, though." She kicked her legs and sat up again. "Tonight is my big date with Josh! For a whole week I've forced myself to concentrate on my mom's visit and my history paper. Well, my mom's gone and my paper's done, so I think I deserve to go a little nu nu."

"Nu nu?" KC questioned.

"You know what I mean. Listen to this." Winnie scrambled across the floor to her carpetbag. After sorting through a mess of three-by-five cards, old candy wrappers, and cassette tapes, she pulled out a scroll of computer paper. "Josh left this tacked to my door, along with a bagel and some erasers shaped like ducks." Winnie flung the paper, which unrolled across the room like a streamer. It was printed with huge dot-matrix letters, only a few words to each page.

*Dear Winnie: This is a techno-request for your presence at a rendezvous (I think that means "date"—you tell me, you're the one who's taking French) on Tuesday night at seven-thirty at Geppetto's Café, just two blocks west of campus, across the street from the infamous Zero Bagel.*

Winnie held up the page. "He drew this crazy little map here." She showed the others Josh's map, then found her place again and continued reading.

*"Can we meet there, since I have a computer-users club meeting at the MicroCenter downtown? I thought of changing our rendezvous when I remembered said techno-nerd meeting, but I also remembered certain hints on your part about my lack of*

*reliability in the past. Since I do not wish to rein-*
*force said misconceptions, I will be sitting at Gep-*
*petto's, on the dot, with my heart on my sleeve,*
*gravy on my tie, and a dopey smile on my face. If*
*any of this presents a problem, let me know.*

*Yours in good faith and absentmindedness, Josh.*

*P.S. Someone has been doing rude things to your*
*door again. The rest of us on your floor agree . . .*
*clean up your act.*

"Winnie, that's a great invitation," KC admitted.

"I agree," seconded Lauren.

"Back off, girls," Winnie teased. "I met him first,
and I'm going out with him this evening . . .
*alone.*"

Everybody laughed, and then it was back to the
soap.

By that night, Winnie was so excited she could
barely catch her breath. She hadn't eaten since
breakfast. She'd changed her clothes four times. She
was desperate for company. But Faith was working
on her independent-study proposal; Lauren was at
the newspaper office; KC had gone to a meeting
of the Young Entrepreneurs club; and Melissa was
at the library. Winnie had ended up having a conversation with one of Melissa's anatomy models.

"My, but you have a beautiful spleen, my dear,"

Winnie chattered. "I know, you must hear that all the time."

For the fifth, and what she decided would be the last, time, Winnie found a new outfit. She put on a sequined skirt she'd bought at the theater-arts department's costume sale, along with a leotard, a man's tie, and floppy boots trimmed with jingle bells. Slipping on a few more bracelets for good luck, she found her keys and checked the clock one last time. It was five after seven, which would give her time to walk to Geppetto's and an extra five minutes to check her hair and makeup when she got there. She was almost out the door when someone called from down the hall, "Winnie Gottleib!"

Winnie looked out. It was Shawna Plimpton, a sophomore party girl who was on the tennis team and had a bronze, sun-lamp tan.

"Hi, Shawna," Winnie called back.

"Where are you going?"

"Out." Winnie grinned.

Shawna lived two doors down from Josh. If this date was going to be the start of something heavy, Winnie figured she should be a little discreet, for once.

"Cool," Shawna nodded. "But you'd better grab the hall phone first. There's a call for you."

"For me?"

"Unless there's another Winnie Gottleib on this

floor." Shawna smiled and disappeared into Todd Beringer's single room.

"A phone call for me," Winnie repeated as she wandered down the hall.

She felt a sudden ache when she passed Josh's door and wondered if he was calling to cancel their date. Wouldn't that be perfect? She was set up with her heart wide open and he was going to tell her that he had just been picked to work on some new programming project that was so important that he wouldn't be able to see her until spring.

But as Winnie brought the receiver to her ear, that dull feeling changed to a hot explosion, a terrifying flying-apart of her emotions that could scatter her all the way to Paris and back. She put her hand to her throat and tried to swallow.

"Hello," she breathed, knowing now that it was Travis.

"Is this Winnie?"

"Oh God," Winnie mouthed. It *was* Travis! His voice was hoarse, almost gravelly from the hours he spent singing over the twang of his electric bass guitar. And he had that lazy, slight, slow drawl, a remnant of a childhood spent in Alabama.

"Hello?"

"This is Winnie." Every instinct Winnie had ever had to run off at the mouth failed her. Her mind became a total blank.

"Hi," he finally said. "This is Travis."

Winnie just stood there.

"Remember me?"

"Oh. Of course. Hi, Travis. Hi."

His mind seemed to have gone blank, too. For the longest time Winnie stood there listening to telephone static and feeling her heart throb. The impact of Travis's voice was so overwhelming that she could barely think or move.

"My mother said you called," he said at last, sounding uncomfortable.

"Yes, I did."

"It's been a while. I guess I'd given up on ever talking to you again." A hint of anger had come into his voice. "So how've you been?"

"Fine."

"How's college?"

"Pretty good." Winnie remembered that Travis hadn't included college in his plans. In Paris he'd talked about "the school of real life." "Your mom said you had a new band. How's that going?"

"We haven't been together too long, but we're starting to cook. We're doing our first demo session next week."

"Really?"

"Yeah."

Winnie was starting to remember more and more about her time with Travis. She thought back to

Travis's tiny second-floor hotel room with the French doors and the balcony that overlooked the street, the sound of car horns and wind, going to sleep while Travis sang his soft, husky lullabies, laughing so hard at a bistro that they were both asked to leave. "Is the demo going to be a song you wrote?"

"Uh-huh." He sighed loudly and there was another pause. "It's a song I wrote about you."

Winnie wanted to crumple at the knees and cry. She wondered if it was a sad song, an angry rock screamer, or a melodic love ballad.

"So, Win, why did you call me after all this time?" Travis asked after another lull. "I don't want to waste our time. I got over you after you didn't answer my letters. You know I'm not into playing games."

"I'm not playing a game."

"Well, something strange happened, Win. I don't hear from you all summer or fall, and all of a sudden you call my mom like we'd just run into each other at the corner store."

"Oh Travis," Winnie gushed.

And then her voice came back. She explained about the letters going to the wrong address and how long it had taken for them to reach her. She admitted that she'd given up on him after assuming that he'd forgotten her and gone on his way. She even told him about college and classes and how she was beginning to get her life together.

After all that talking, it was hard to stop—until Winnie caught a glimpse of the hall clock and felt her stomach shoot down to her toes. *It was after seven-thirty!* Somehow she'd been on the phone with Travis for half an hour.

"Travis, it's wonderful to talk to you again," she panicked, "but I have to go. I have a . . . class."

"Okay, Win," he said so slowly that it almost drove her wild. "We'll talk again. Now that we've found each other again, we can't lose touch."

"We won't. We won't. I promise. Now goodbye."

She hung up the phone before Travis could even say goodbye and took off, almost stumbling down the hall. She ran through the crowd in the lobby, out the front stairs, and across the green.

Cutting through the dorm parking lot, Winnie recklessly dodged cars until she hit the street. Then she raced furiously, as if her life depended on it. She barely felt her lungs sting and her legs cramp. She ran through red lights and flew across streets and up and down alleys. When Geppetto's Café was finally in sight she was breathing so hard that she was ready to choke.

Winnie ran into the restaurant, certain that she looked like a red-faced maniac. She looked at every customer at every table. She checked the pay phones and the alley in back and the kitchen. She even considered checking the men's bathroom, but stopped herself before she did something really dumb.

Finally she grabbed a waiter and managed to speak. "Have you seen a college guy, with sort of longish hair and one tiny earring? You might not have even noticed the earring, but he was by himself, waiting for someone. Um, me, to be exact. He was waiting for me. Is he still here?"

The waiter removed Winnie's hands from his jacket and checked the reservation list. He had a long gray mustache, which he plucked as he looked at her.

"Do you mean Josh Gaffey?" he said in a rather bored voice.

"Yes! Josh, yes! Then he's still here?"

"Sorry," the waiter said, giving Winnie a sigh. "He left about ten minutes ago."

"What?" Winnie gasped.

The waiter shrugged. "I think he said he'd waited long enough. Is he a friend of yours or something?"

"Yes."

"Too bad," the waiter answered. "I guess that's the way you lose friends." Then he walked past Winnie and out of the room.

Winnie turned. She felt dizzy. She felt sick to her stomach. She knocked against one of the tables and the silverware rattled. She tried to make herself walk toward the front door, but it was hard. Her eyes were cloudy with tears and she was shaking.

"Are you all right?" a customer at the counter asked her as she stumbled past.

Winnie couldn't answer.

# Fourteen

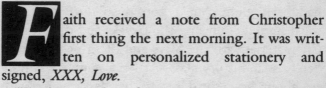

**F**aith received a note from Christopher first thing the next morning. It was written on personalized stationery and signed, *XXX, Love.*

"I'm late, I'm late, for a very important date," she muttered as she crossed the dorm green. Christopher's note was still in her jeans pocket and every word he'd written was imprinted on her brain. "I'll pick you up at your room tonight at seven. Jamie says we'll definitely have the cabin all to ourselves. I've missed you. I can't wait to see you. XXX, Love," Faith recited. Then she shook her head. "Oh, great. I'm starting to talk to myself in public. I'm getting to be as flakey as Winnie."

Faith strode past the dining commons, where she caught a glimpse of her reflection in the double glass doors. "If only I could have been as honest as Winnie, or as brave as Lauren or KC."

She had just come from a Western Civ study session with Winnie, KC, and Lauren. They'd huddled over their textbooks in KC's single room, while KC had decided finally to stick family photos on her wall. Until that morning, KC's room had been a decorating blank, without one souvenir or postcard or photo from home.

While KC had happily tacked and taped, Winnie had been glum. She'd gotten so distraught that she'd started confusing the Greeks and the Western Civ material with the Slavs and other peoples from her Russian-history class. At least Winnie was honest about how she'd blown her last chance with Josh. She admitted that it was all her fault. The whole time, KC had admitted to some major screwups, too. Meanwhile, Lauren told Winnie that facing what she'd done wrong was the first step toward change.

As Faith passed the new computer center and the path that led to Mill Pond, she knew that she had to stop blocking things out and really think about her life. For once, she had to think honestly about her friends. She had to think honestly about her family. She had to think about her independent study. And she had to think about change and herself and facing things that felt wrong.

"I'm late, I'm late," Faith whispered to herself again. "For a very important . . ." Faith knew she really had to think about facing Christopher. She'd put it off long enough.

She kept walking, straight ahead, until she realized that she was in front of the stone steps that led to the University Theater. She stared up at the old building with the Latin phrases over the door.

So far at U of S, the only thing Faith felt really good about was her contribution to the musical *Stop the World, I Want to Get Off.* She'd assisted Christopher, a hard job, and she'd done well. She hadn't avoided the problems or tried to sugar-coat anything. She'd faced the difficulties head-on and overcome them.

The front doors to the theater were locked, so Faith went around to the back where tech people were painting and hammering in the scenery shop. She spotted a dark-haired, teddy-bearish fellow with a baseball cap over his eyes slopping paint on canvas flat. It was her theater friend, Merideth, the sophomore who'd served as stage manager for *Stop the World*.

"Merideth!" Faith called out.

She made her way over to him, squeezing between two old set pieces she recognized from their musical.

"What's going on?"

"Not a thing," Merideth grumbled. He put down his paintbrush, readjusted his glasses, and checked his Mickey Mouse watch. "I'm so bored I even offered to help paint sets for the fall modern-dance performance."

"I didn't know you were interested in modern dance."

"I'm not. I hate it. All those people prancing around waving banners and looking so serious. It makes me nervous."

Faith laughed.

"But there's nothing much going on in the theater-arts department until after Thanksgiving. Just Professor Cohen's production of *Old Times.*"

"Didn't he want you to be the stage manager?"

"*Old Times* is Cohen's pet project. He's using only grad students." Meredith wiped his brow, smearing paint across his forehead. "I guess it's my chance to catch up on my homework for linguistics." He winked. "And if you don't think that's a scintillating class, you have another thing coming."

"Maybe something else will open up soon," Faith suggested.

"I hope so. Otherwise I'm thinking of quitting

school and joining the circus." He smacked his hands together, then went back to his painting.

Faith watched him for a while. "Merideth, have you seen Christopher this morning?"

"Sir Christopher?" Merideth scoffed. "You're not still hanging around with him, are you? You deserve better than having to meet him in dark alleys."

Faith stopped breathing for a moment. During *Stop the World* Faith had assumed that her relationship with Christopher was a secret. In rehearsals they'd made sure to treat each other with business-like formality. But she'd suspected that Merideth knew something was going on between them.

"Was it obvious that I was hanging around with him?"

"Everyone knew."

"They did?"

"Faith, Christopher's romances are never that big a secret."

Faith wanted to curl up and bury herself in a pile of sawdust. "I must be the densest freshman alive."

Merideth reached back to pat her. "Don't take it too hard. Christopher also has very good taste."

Faith was beginning to wonder how many other girls Christopher had been seeing while he was engaged to Suzanna. Two? Twelve? "So you don't know where he is?"

"I think he goes down to the TV station on Wednesday mornings. You could check there."

"Thanks." Faith started to leave.

Before she even reached the loading dock, however, she froze. Her mind was starting to function again. It was as if facing the truth about Christopher had opened up more space in her brain for other things.

"Merideth," she called back, "if I came up with a theater project, an independent study, would you work on it with me?"

"Sure. You know I would."

"Really?" She waved and began to run. "Great," she said as she dodged two techies carrying armfuls of lighting instruments. "Sorry," she gasped, sidestepping them and racing back out, back past Mill Pond and the computer center and across the green.

Faith ran for seven straight blocks. She didn't get winded. Her legs didn't ache. By the time she reached the TV station, on the edge of downtown, she was feeling even stronger and more clear.

Set in a block of nondescript warehouses, the KRUS TV-station building was low and wide. It looked about as glamorous as a concrete block. Faith pushed her way through the double glass doors and found a plain lobby where a pretty, college-age receptionist sat eating a container of yogurt.

"Can I help you?" the receptionist asked in a bored voice.

When Faith didn't answer right away she went back to her yogurt and a letter she was writing on her desk.

"I'm looking for someone who's an intern here," Faith managed, even though she was suddenly overcome by doubt again. She couldn't go barging into the TV station. What if Christopher was in the middle of a news broadcast?

"Which intern?"

Luckily, Faith didn't need to say another word, because she spotted him. He was on the other side of a big glass pane, talking with an older man, nodding intently as if he were receiving important instructions. Faith had been afraid that she would crumble as soon as she saw Christopher's handsome face again. Instead, watching him ooze his elegant, dishonest charm made her want to break through the glass, grab him by the collar, and shake him.

A moment later, the door behind the reception desk opened and the older man led Christopher out.

"Good work, Chris," the man said. "If you keep on like this, you'll have a future here."

"Thank you, sir."

"See you on Friday."

As Christopher turned to leave, the slick charm fell off his face. He looked right at Faith and for a moment didn't seem to quite remember who she was.

Faith walked up to him. "We need to talk. Shall we talk here, or do you want to go outside?"

Putting his Mr. Charm smile back on, Christopher glanced back at the receptionist. "Sure. I didn't expect to see you until tonight. Why don't you walk me to my car?"

He held the door open for Faith and they went outside. The sky and the buildings looked gray.

"I know you didn't expect to see me before tonight," Faith said, striding alongside him. She was surprised at her no-nonsense tone. "You probably didn't want to see me before tonight. But I wanted to see you. I needed to see you."

"Okay. Is this about tonight? You can still come to the cabin, can't you?"

Faith cut him off. "Just listen to what I have to say, Christopher. It won't take long."

They reached his little sports car. He opened the door to toss in his jacket, then jumped up to sit on the hood. His cuffs were rolled up and his tie was loose. He'd put on his easy smile again.

"What is it?" he asked, assuming his old, intimate tone. "Did you want to find out about Suzanna?"

For a moment, Faith felt the old pull. "Sure," she said flatly. "Tell me about Suzanna."

He reached out for Faith. "It's over. I told you I'd end it and I did. Ask anybody. Didn't I tell you that you could trust me?"

Faith didn't fall for it this time. There was only a mere memory of her old desire to fall into his arms. She pushed his arms away. "But I *don't* trust you, Christopher. How can I trust you when you've lied to me every step of the way."

"I haven't lied to you! I broke off my engagement, just like I said I would. I did that for you."

"You didn't do that for me, Christopher. You did it for the same person you do everything for—yourself."

He grabbed her arms. "You have a lot of nerve saying this to me after I broke up with the woman I was supposed to marry because of you."

"Was it really because of me? Or was it because of that girl you were kissing at your frat party Saturday night? Or maybe it was because of some other girl that I don't even know about."

For the first time all trace of ease and confidence left Christopher's face.

"What girl at my frat house?" he said weakly.

"The one my friend KC saw you with."

His face went pale.

"I was lonely," he began to ramble. "I was upset.

Suzanna didn't take the breakup very well. You weren't there when I needed you."

"Have you ever been there when I needed you, Christopher? Would you ever be there when I needed you?"

He reached out for her again but she backed away.

"Oh, Christopher," Faith said with growing confidence. "I wanted any excuse to trust you, to think that you really cared about me and were an okay guy." She paused. "But I can't pretend anymore. You're nothing but a liar and a slime. So you see, there's no way I'm going to Jamie's cabin with you, tonight or any other night."

Faith turned and began to walk away.

Christopher jumped off the car hood and ran after her. When she pulled away from him again, he dodged into the street, almost running into a car. When he caught up with her and blocked her path, Faith saw something new in his face—true desperation.

"Faith, I'm sorry," he panted. "I can't help it. I'm scared. Suzanna scared me. You scare me. I think sometimes that you want something I don't know how to give. It isn't that I don't love you."

"You love me?" she spat back.

"I love you. I love the old, sweet, naive Faith.

Don't you remember anything that's gone on between us?"

"I'm afraid I don't remember," Faith said, turning away and leaving him on the sidewalk. "Because, Christopher, all of that happened to a totally different girl."

Instead of being alone with Christopher that evening, the new Faith was with Lauren and her old friends. The four of them had discovered a new hangout: Hondo's Café, just off campus. It was the essential college joint, with sawdust on the floor and pennants on the walls, flashy old jukeboxes, sloppy submarine sandwiches, and loud, happy chatter. The place was packed and it looked like every customer there was a student at U of S.

"Now, Faith, isn't this better than spending the night with two-timing Christopher in some dreary old cabin?" KC teased.

Faith laughed. The Hondo's Café looked great to her. She no longer felt either naive or sophisticated. The goofy, semi-grown-up college atmosphere suited her perfectly.

"I've decided that anything is better than spending this evening with a guy," Winnie grumbled. "I'm sure glad the three of you are here."

"It's good for all of us to be together again," KC admitted.

Lauren nodded and smiled.

They all dug into their subs, passing tastes around the table, removing onions, adding mustard, taking big gushy bites that made tomato juice run down their chins.

"So, Faith," Lauren brought up, "your advisor really approved your *Alice in Wonderland* idea?"

"He did? What did he say?" Winnie gasped.

Faith took a huge gulp of soda. She grinned. "I was amazed, because I didn't have my idea written out. I went right over to my advisor's office after telling Christopher off. I was still so fired up, I thought my advisor would think I was acting like a maniac."

"Sounds familiar," Winnie said.

Faith patted Winnie. "But I guess he thought I was just passionate about my idea. Actually, I was. Anyway, he let me explain it."

"What is your idea?" asked Lauren.

Faith ripped open a bag of chips. "I want to do an experimental version of *Alice in Wonderland*, using a few kids from the day-care center, but mainly using students from the theater-arts department who aren't too busy right now. I described how I wanted to work on scenes, with actors not only playing the characters but also playing the flowers and the furniture. I even told my advisor about the Dormouse exercise we did at the day-care center and my ideas about having five different actors play different parts of one character."

"Wow," commented KC.

"I think it sounds great," agreed Lauren.

"I guess my advisor thought so, too." Faith grinned. "He said yes! I still have to write the whole thing out in a formal proposal, but as long as I do that, I can start my independent-study project!"

Winnie raised a curl of tomato and wiggled it over the table. Then she pounded her fist on the bench. "Let's eat a sub to that. Even though I'm about ready to lose my mind, I still feel like celebrating. I can celebrate for *Alice in Wonderland,* and for having found Travis again. That'll help me forget how I totally ruined things with Josh."

KC hugged Winnie and agreed. "Look at the bright side. We survived Parents' Visit."

"We did," said Faith, raising a piece of salami.

Lauren waved a shred of lettuce. "Dash and I got our story."

Winnie held up a hot pepper. "Faith is about to become the darling of the theater world."

"And we're all about to face midterms," KC reminded them. Her announcement was greeted by a chorus of boos.

The four friends then continued to stuff themselves and to talk at the same time. Faith went over her breakup with Christopher at least five more

212     •     *Linda A. Cooney*

times, while Lauren told and retold her and Dash's rescue of Howard Benmann. Winnie decided that for that night, at least, she wasn't going to think about Josh, and KC invited them all to go home to her parents' restaurant for Thanksgiving—providing they all aced their midterms.

Soon it was late, and even though the café was still hopping, Faith was eager to get home and work on her independent-study proposal. She pushed back her chair and made her way through the sawdust and the students, hoping to find their waitress and total up their bill.

"Excuse me," she said, squeezing past a nice-looking guy with blond ringlets who was sticking quarters in the jukebox.

He turned and looked right at her. "Hi, Faith."

There was no déjà vu this time. Faith had no confusion or thoughts of Christopher. She knew instantly that it was Brooks. "Hi."

"How are you?" Brooks asked in a tentative voice, pushing his curls off his forehead. He tried to look discreetly past her to see whom she was sitting with.

"I'm not with Christopher," Faith stated. "I'm with Winnie, KC, and Lauren."

"Oh." He leaned back against the jukebox, scuffing a hiking boot along the floor. "I mean, it's none of my business."

"That's okay. Christopher and I broke up."

"Actually, I've been feeling like I owe you an apology. I came down pretty hard on you during Parents' Visit."

"I deserved it. A little."

Brooks shrugged. "Maybe I'm still hurt over what happened between us. But I'm getting over it."

Faith smiled and faced him. "It's okay, Brooks."

"I know."

Brooks looked away, as if he weren't sure whether to walk away or what to do next. A new song came on the jukebox, an oldie that was mellow and slow.

"Anyway, it's good to see you," Faith said.

"You, too."

Faith started to walk away, then stopped. She took a step up to Brooks and gave him a warm, friendly hug.

Brooks hugged her back.

"It's okay, Brooks," Faith said, after she pulled away. Brooks's face was flushed, but Faith felt brave and strong. "Things change."

*Here's a sneak preview of*
Freshman Dreams, *the fifth*
book in the compelling story
of FRESHMAN DORM.

*I*t was nearly midnight. Winnie sat cradled in Travis's lap in a small park on the edge of downtown Springfield. The park was silent, and Winnie thought she could almost hear her heart beating.

The whole afternoon and evening had been incredible. Travis took Winnie to the old Springfield train station and to a greenhouse that grew orchids. They talked to people they didn't know in parks, on buses, and on the streets. They ate lunch at an open-air market in the run-down northern district, sampling nuts and cinnamon rolls, beef jerky and spice tea. They walked and walked, and talked and talked.

"I just can't believe that this town has so many amazing things in it, and all I know about is the university."

"I think that's why I decided not to go to college," Travis said. They both got up and began to stroll, hand in hand. "They make you think you're enlarging your world, but you're not. You don't find out about anything except what they tell you in the classroom. And as far as I'm concerned, there's a lot more than what's in books and on blackboards."

"I know what you're saying, and I agree with you . . . sort of," Winnie said. "But you can learn things in a classroom, too. Right now I'm taking two history classes, and Western Civ. It all makes me feel like I understand the world a little better. Does that make sense?"

"Maybe. Except you don't have to be in a classroom to learn all that. You could just read books on your own. I learned to write songs and to play the guitar through books and by listening to records. I never took a real lesson."

They stopped in front of the boarding house where Travis had rented a room. It was a dingy two-story house with a Rooms for Rent sign out front. Slowly they walked up the steps, lingering at the door. Travis put his hands on Winnie's shoulders, then ran his palms slowly down her arms. He began to kiss her, lightly, on her forehead, her cheeks, her neck.

"Oh, Win," he whispered.

Winnie allowed her real world to disappear again. The dingy porch, midterms, grades, and Josh were all forgotten as Travis's long, deep kisses made her whole body feel as if it was floating. When they broke apart, Winnie was flooded with memories of Paris, memories of staying with Travis in his little hotel. Travis had been her first lover. Her only lover. When she thought back to that now, she wasn't sure why she had chosen him to be first, of what that huge step in their relationship had meant.

He reached for the front door. "Come on up to my room," Travis whispered. "If we sneak past the front desk, they won't see you."

Winnie started for the door, but then something stopped her. It was the memory of how hurt she had been when Travis had left Paris, and the thought that he would eventually leave Springfield, too. Now that the dizzying kisses had stopped, Winnie also remembered the pressure of her exams —and Josh. She hung back on the porch.

Travis gave her a confused look.

"It's really late," Winnie said. "I should get back to the dorms while the buses are still running. I have my French midterm tomorrow."

"So we'll speak French to each other," he wooed.

Winnie looked away. "Travis, you don't speak French."

"So teach me." He took her hands and looked at her. "You either know the stuff or you don't, Win. If you ask me, college is for the birds. I don't know how you can take it all seriously."

Winnie thought for a moment. Was she really serious about college? She realized that she was. "I have to, Travis. College is my future."

Travis looked angry. "College isn't your future," he argued. "You don't know what your future is. Are you going to be one of those people who plans out their life when they're eighteen and dies of boredom at thirty? Where's the impulsive Winnie I knew in Europe?"

"She's still here. I guess she just lives with another Winnie now, one that's a tiny bit more cautious."

"Caution is for old people, Win." Travis looked into her eyes for a long time.